IF ONLY THEY KNEW

a collection of short stories

by Madeline Trionfo

IF ONLY THEY KNEW
a short story collection

Copyright © 2021 Madeline Trionfo

Cover design by John Trionfo, Jr.

Print ISBN: 978-1-66782-5-434
eBook ISBN: 978-1-66782-5-441

CONTENTS

The Neighbors

CHAPTER 1

A Short Conversation

HE SAID, "THIS HILL IN YOUR BACKYARD IS VERY STEEP ... twenty feet high I would guess. You could charge children to sled down it in the winter!"

She thought, *Charge children? Sled?*

She said, "This is Virginia, Russ. Snow? Charge children? If I were so inclined, children would not be charged, if we had snow that is. It might snow once, maybe twice, never more than an inch and it melts by noon. You've lived across the street for three years; haven't you noticed? This isn't central Pennsylvania."

She thought, *Why are you here, in my back yard? The only time we see each other is by circumstance when getting the newspaper, the mail, or moving trash cans back and forth from the curb. Have we ever had a conversation before? I don't think so. And, yet, here you are, talking about snow, children, and my steep hill.*

Her response was marked with impatience as she snapped, "What do you want?"

Russ hemmed and hawed. When he started to speak, Rose came closer to him and said, "I wouldn't want children on my property! And sledding? With all their excited screaming? Never! I don't like them."

"You don't like children? Weren't you a school teacher before you retired?"

3

"I was paid to like them for 180 days a year as a teacher's aide. It was a survival technique. I took pills everyday to help me cope. Damn pills; stopped them after nine years and got a different job." Rose paused to catch her breath as Russ turned abruptly and left.

CHAPTER 2

Toni

———

I LIVE ON A CUL-DE-SAC WITH LARGE LOTS AND HUMBLE brick bungalows dating from the time when sensibly priced houses were in demand. Sugar maples line the road, providing shade and color that enriches our lane with dignity and a sense of Americana. Our street looks welcoming as it circles about and forces drivers to slow down, giving them more time to notice window boxes, neatly edged driveways and sidewalks, and front porches with swings or rocking chairs.

However, welcoming does not describe the inhabitants who favor minding their own business and expecting everyone to do likewise, waving perhaps to assure a bottom-line approach to being cordial. If, by accident eye contact occurs, head nodding is the typical greeting along with the ubiquitous, "Hi, how are you?" and not wanting an answer because it might lead to conversation. I like it this way.

Things changed the day Rose knocked on my door. I was surprised when, after opening the door, she entered as if this was normal behavior. I finished buttoning my oversize plaid flannel shirt as she sat down and told me about her conversation with Russ. She said, " 'Charge children!' He actually said that. Who would think of doing such an outrageous thing?"

Slender hands gesticulated; cheap bracelets jingled in response. She pulled on strands of her long graying hair while I twisted a rubber band around mine. She babbled the entire time, then drummed long, unpainted fingernails on the table top. She was making me nervous.

"Rose, focus. Calm down!"

With a small child-like voice she murmured, "I don't want to be like her. I am trying so hard. I'll try harder, if you listen."

I didn't ask about "her." I did not want to encourage conversation in which I would be expected to offer solutions or solace.

Her words came swiftly now, her entire body shifting back and forth as perspiration formed under her dark eyes. I became concerned. Placing my hand on her shoulder I whispered, "Breathe." Her rigid body did not respond. Reluctantly, I pulled out a chair and got her a glass of water.

"Toni, he is silly, talking about children and snow." I sat down and she told me about their brief conversation.

"Rose, he didn't mean any harm, right?" I was guessing here, feeling uncomfortable, not knowing either Rose or Russ well enough to form an opinion.

"I can't let this go."

I said, "You should."

She said, "I won't."

I hesitated before asking, "Why?"

"Because I wanted to say more and he walked away! He made me feel like a wicked, nasty old woman with a wart on my nose."

I was ready to turn and leave, fearing too much involvement in this bizarre event; but I couldn't leave. We were in *my* kitchen!

I stood, walked to the door and hoped that she was smart enough to take the hint. She wasn't. She put both hands on her face and I feared she might cry.

"Rose, I have a doctor's appointment," and I opened the door.

Two weeks later, Rose was charged with "intent to do bodily harm." She was found guilty and fined $1,000.00. The police were holding her in a small facility adjoining the court house until the fine was paid.

She called me and I went to the holding cell. She expected that I would pay her bail.

I said, "Sorry, I can't help you. My hours have been cut at the store. I would if I could." Then I added, "Russ is doing much better. He's on antibiotics."

"Antibiotics for poison ivy? Never heard of that," she said.

"I never said it was for poison ivy, Rose."

The familiar distractions began as she entered a zone of confusion— rapid eye blinks matched by shirt tugging and foot tapping.

"Most of his body was covered. As a matter of fact, his back was the only clear area. The doctor said the blisters were large and looked infected. Russ has no idea how this happened. He can't wear shoes or even socks and is determined, when he is able, to find where it is growing in his flowerbeds. He thinks you were arrested for that incident last week when a neighbor's car had a punctured tire. We all knew about your complaining and your threats because of the Dawson's barking dog and the mess left in your yard. Did you do that, Rose, puncture their tire?"

Not answering my question, Rose became agitated, moving about her cell, hand wringing and head bobbing. A quick turn and a smile appeared on her face.

She said, "You mean Russ has no idea *I* gave him poison ivy? How can that be? I thought he filed charges? Why am I here?"

And there it was. Confession by way of assumption!

"Because *I* called the sheriff. You have a record, Rose. You know that. Twice, the police have been to our neighborhood because of you. I'm thinking there must be more, like maybe you have had other issues with the law, because when I reported my suspicions the police took it seriously enough to react. I saw them come to your house. Couldn't stop yourself, could you? I'm betting you got riled up when they questioned you. Sometimes you are your worst enemy, Rose. You talk too much. You tangle yourself into a wordy knot. I'm guessing you confessed. You owe me an explanation. I know why you did it. I want to know how you did it."

She started tugging at her clothes. Then lowered her head, raised it up high, thrust her chin out, and looked defiant.

"Why should I tell you? If you aren't going to help me, why are you here?"

"Because there is another option. It is in your best interest to talk."

"In that case, I'll satisfy your curiosity. Poison ivy was twisting its ugly way up my oak tree. I was spraying it when my malicious mind, "deliciously malicious" my mother used to say, tumbled through scenarios to teach Russ a lesson. No, that's not true. It's about revenge. That damn conversation, I couldn't let it go. It became an obsession, which I do have; can't always control myself."

Obviously, I thought.

She whispered rhyming words, talked to her self, forgot I was there: "delicious and malicious, perseverate and degenerate"…a pause then "resolution, no solution, proposition, opposition." I waited. Five minutes later she blinked, stared at me, and then continued. "I filled in the blanks of my thinking as I watched him hang out his laundry, all of those long-sleeved, button-down collared shirts and khaki pants. Doesn't he have a dryer like everybody else? His clothes never look wrinkled. Does he iron, actually own an ironing board like our mothers used?"

"I'm confused," I interrupted. "You're rambling I think. Does this matter? Help me to understand."

"I confuse you? I'll amuse you, or defuse you, or refuse to!"

"ROSE!"

"Sorry, Toni. I filled a bag with the poison ivy and rubbed the leaves all over his clothes as they dried in his backyard. I was careful not to be seen. I waited for him to leave the house. No one was outside. Yours was the only car on the driveway. I think. I can't remember. There were too many thoughts. A doctor's words echoed as I did the dirty deed, 'consider the consequences'… over and over again until I wanted to scream! I like his detergent, Toni. I must find out what he uses."

She really needs help.

We heard someone approaching the holding cells with keys clanging and calling out, "Which one of you is The Itch?"

A raspy voice answered, "I am! I'm the bitch, officer! Did you say bitch?"

"Go back to sleep, Wanda. Your friend is on her way to get you outta here…again."

The guard saw me and his jaw tightened as he placed a hand near his stun gun.

"Why are you here instead of the visitor center?"

I pulled out $50.00 and handed it to him stating, "This is how. Your coworker liked the idea."

"It works for me," he replied, snatched the money and unlocked the door, saying, "Let's go Miss Itch; the judge wants to see you."

"WAIT! Just one damn moment! Hours cut? Can't help a neighbor? One hundred dollars in cash! You had $100.00 for the guards."

From my pocket, I withdrew a wad of bills which totaled $900.00 and handed it to her. I said, "Here, Russ wants to help you. I want him not to. I needed to see you, thinking you would be miserable and regretting what you did. You aren't. You're short $100.00 for your 'Get out of Jail Free Card.' Figure it out."

By the time I picked up groceries and arrived home, a cab was dropping her off. Russ, wrapped in cotton strips over arms and legs was on his front steps smiling and waving an enthusiastic "hello" to her. She looked his way then turned and went into the house.

I wish I had told Russ about my suspicions before accepting his $1,000.00. When I asked him why he wanted to help Rose, he shrugged his shoulders and said, "Please do this for me."

Was he attracted to Rose? Are they both crazy? Go figure, if you dare, to comprehend the human heart when opposites attract, or don't, or when it's one-sided.

CHAPTER 3

Martha

MARTHA TOOK THE NEWBORN HOME WITHOUT HAVING given her a name. She exerted enough pressure at the hospital by exhibiting disturbing behaviors: shouting, flailing her arms and tugging at her hair until they relented 'for the good of the mother's health.'

"Non compos mentis," a doctor whispered to his staff, "to be included on baby's record along with the notation 'unnamed female infant.' "

Martha had perfected what she thought of as 'workable characteristics' over the course of a life not well lived. She thought they helped her to avoid arrest and find understanding pimps. She failed on both counts. "I was born this way," was her conceit. And she nourished those attributes to bully and demean anyone who got in her way.

At home, snuggling the infant, Martha smiled as she pried open tiny fists, fitting her finger inside.

"She loves me so much. She squeezes with such strength. Determined, aren't you my pretty? Only one of us can be in charge and that would be me," she whispered and kissed the baby's forehead.

Peering at the puckering mouth, searching, rooting at Martha's shirt, sucking at Martha's finger as soon as it was offered, the hungry infant became seven pounds of thrashing limbs. Martha traced the flesh of the infant's lips, stopping at the small mound centered on the top lip, like a rosebud that would one day flower into a young lady. She wrapped the infant tighter, subduing her movements, and then placed her upon the bed. Humming and prancing around the area, Martha withdrew the Ruby Red lipstick from her purse and painted the baby's lips.

"Razzle Dazzle Rose, Razzle Dazzle, Rose! Razzle and Dazzle," she sang repeatedly, even as the hungry baby cried.

CHAPTER 4

Rose

———

ROSE SLOUCHED HER WAY INTO THE GUIDANCE COUNSELOR'S office of her high school, tossed her backpack on the floor, and pulled up the chair that she felt was too far away for the close contact she liked when making a point.

"I need a place to stay. Everything I own is in this backpack and if you can't help me, I'll be on the street after dismissal. Don't look at me like that. Aren't you supposed to help me? A teacher told me to come see you but I don't have the time to explain. You'd understand if only you knew what I've been through." Rose laughed loudly, stretched her right arm up and over to pat herself on the back. "I'm a poet, Miss Bracker! If only you *knew* what I've been *through*," she repeated with emphasis. " Here's the thing: I will steal to survive. I know how to do that. My mother taught me. What do you say, Miss Bracker?"

"Who are you? And do you have an appointment?" Miss Bracker asked leaning over a stack of paperwork.

"Oops, I guess I'll leave. I need guidance now." And with that, Rose grabbed her bag and left the office.

She was stopped at the door by a teacher on duty to check the early leave passes and began to explain when Miss Bracker called to her and asked if she would return to talk. The result put Rose into foster care and Martha into court and eventually to the County Women's Correctional Facility.

By the time she was twenty-one, Rose was employed by a reputable temporary employment service to interview and place people with office skills. Wages hovered above the minimum level, yet she lived in a high-rise condo, drove an expensive car, and wore stylish clothes. Rose was good at her job but better at stealing, sometimes grifting with one friend or another. Men were attracted by her dark-brown eyes set in a delicate-looking face and honey-colored hair that moved in soft waves, ebbing and flowing with every turn of her head. She flaunted her height by keeping her shoulders back and her jaw angled to catch the light on high cheekbones. She smiled and encouraged compliments, sometimes crude ones. She discouraged any attempts when offers to date were expressed. Outside, she exuded confidence; inside, she seethed.

Being arrested was the first good thing that happened to her. Rose was able to make a deal for leniency by revealing names and dates to the authorities, who considered her the least dangerous of a group that was wanted for small-time robberies and aggravated assaults.

"You're lucky, Rose, to have been granted a plea deal. Don't waste this opportunity. What are your plans?" Her attorney asked.

"To get the hell out of Dodge. I'm not doing this anymore. Trust me, I can change," she replied while tugging off her high heels and putting on tennis shoes.

"Yeah, sure Rose. That's what they all say."

CHAPTER 5

The Dinner

TWO WEEKS AFTER HER BAIL WAS POSTED, ROSE ASKED IF I could come over. She needed my help, my input, and she needed it immediately. She sounded desperate, but then she usually does.

"What?" I asked impatiently as she opened the door to her kitchen. My hair was tied up in my grandmother's bandana, my bib jeans had two rags hanging from pockets, and I smelled of vinegar, which really is the best way to clean windows.

Rose looked good, pretty almost, wearing white jeans and a tank top with large hoop earrings. Her hair was neatly combed with a deep wave finding its way down her left cheek. She smiled. She also looked taller and I wondered why I had not noticed this before.

"Sit, please, and have some ice tea. With or without sugar?" in a singsong voice.

"I'm busy; get to the point, Rose. And no ice tea. I won't be here long enough to drink it."

She poured it anyway, placed the sugar bowl and spoon in front of me, pulled a chair close to mine and sat. Her right arm crept around me and rested on the back of my chair. Taking a deep breath, I wondered what this meant. But not for long as I pushed my chair back, got up and walked to the opposite side of the table. "Rose," I said, "Why am I here?"

"I want to invite Russ for dinner and I need you to come too."

I sank into a chair and added sugar to the tea I didn't want. Damn it!

"Russ? Dinner? Need? No!"

"Let me explain," she started.

Her body tensed as she saw me get up and walk toward the door.

"Toni, I am not a good person. What I did was horrible. He must never, ever know. Maybe I can atone and he will forgive me."

"How can he forgive you if he doesn't know what you did, Rose? On what level is your brain operating? That poison ivy stunt was malicious and comes from a mind that scares me."

"I want to change."

"And I want to leave."

"Toni, I'm trying. I don't want to be like her. My mother was a psychopath, and I carry her scars."

"If you invited me here to blame your actions on a bad childhood, you asked the wrong person. Look, Rose, I had a chaotic childhood too, but I decided to take responsibility for my actions. And do you know why? Because I'm an adult! Grow up and stop blaming your mother. Oh, and I'll give you the name of my therapist."

"Help me and I'll see your therapist. I am guilty of disgusting and cruel behavior, and I wish I had not caused Russ so much pain. He didn't deserve to suffer. I need you, I need to be able to sleep, and I need another person to make my dinner work. I will try to behave and enjoy his company. I was mean to punish him when he didn't do anything. Please, Toni, won't you help me?"

Before I could leave, she did. Her chair fell backward as she made a dash down a hallway, shouting, "Wait! My pants are too short, my underwear too tight, and my bra uncomfortable! Wait! Please wait until I change clothes. Five minutes, give me five minutes."

Her voice trailed off as the screen door slammed and I ran home.

Sunday, late afternoon, I sat reading on my front porch. I saw Russ carrying flowers as he crossed the street to Rose's house. I made the sign of the cross, whispered to one of the friendly deities, crossed my fingers, and would have thrown salt over my shoulder too. This could go sideways, a disaster looming, and I was not going inside until Russ came outside, which I hoped would be in a few minutes.

Three hours later, as street lights were coming on, he emerged, then turned and blew a kiss back to her. I visualized a halo hovering above him as he entered into the arc of the overhead light. He must have sensed being watched, then turned in my direction. I pulled deeper into the swing to be concealed by my large hydrangea.

"Hi, Toni," he called. "Lovely evening, isn't it?"

Next morning I crossed the street to Rose's house.

I could smell fresh coffee brewing as she opened the door in a pink, chenille bathrobe.

"Did you poison him this time?"

"Not funny and not yet!" Then seeing my eyes widen, "Just kidding!"

Rose hummed as she poured two dark cups.

"Glad you're wearing comfortable clothes, Rose. Nothing binding you, right?"

"Yea, sorry about running away from you, really had to change my clothes! It's been a problem for me. My mother use to swaddle me, tightly, even when I was no longer a newborn. Certain things stick, adhere to my inner self. Making progress though, not blaming my mother."

Sympathy pricked my spine. I was not sure how much I could absorb. I sensed she was going off into a torturous review of her childhood. Not good for her, and terrible for me, so I interrupted. "I saw Russ leaving last night. I feel obligated to pry, to not mind my own business. You involved me already and I helped. You know I feel concerned about him. What is happening? Will detectives be knocking on my door? Is jail in your future? Just tell me everything is normal so I can leave."

She poured herself a second cup, drank it, and poured another. Small beads of perspiration on her upper lip, nails tap, tap, tapping on the table, bathrobe being loosened and a deep inhaling warned me to prepare myself.

"We're getting married. We love each other."

I grabbed the edge of the table. The Broca area of the brain is located in the frontal lobe and is responsible for speech production. Mine wasn't working. Words were caught between Broca area and mouth, which is responsible for actually saying the damn words that I could not find!

She brewed more coffee, fanned herself with the newspaper, removed her robe and provided more details about last evening.

She put donuts and fruit on the table then refreshed my coffee, saying, "I'm so glad you dropped by. We've been close, don't you think? Friends? No? Ok. Neighbors, good neighbors. Right?"

I was reaching a nasty conclusion: *Married? A wedding?* I whispered, "You're not going to ask me to be your…"

She interrupted, "Toni, will you please…"

"NO!" My volume surprised me as I feared she would say, "*Be my bridesmaid?*"

She said, "Pass the sugar?"

CHAPTER 6

Friends

_____

RUSS AND ROSE WERE MARRIED THAT SUMMER. THE CERE-
mony was held in Russ' backyard, where they created a lush garden area filled
with ferns and hostas. Off the path and in a quiet corner, a small fountain
near a koi pond gurgled its way over polished, gray stones creating a mood
for quiet meditation. The canopy of large deciduous trees allowed shafts
of sunlight to dapple the greenery, changing it to various shades and hues.
Jack-in-the-Pulpits, always one of my favorites, filled a large area surround-
ing elegant, black bamboo once photographed for an article in our local
newspaper. Russ told everyone how happy it made him to have Rose's help
in designing the idyllic landscape.

"I like dirt," she announced. "Won't wear gloves because I like the way
it feels. I like digging holes, too, deep ones. Russ bought me work boots and
my own spade and the deeper the hole, the better I feel. Tiny little plants, like
newborns, are dependent on me to nourish them. I cut their flowers or pick
their fruit and make myself tired and messy working in the garden. Here's
the gift: I get a great night's sleep!"

How could have I been so wrong? Can people change? Or was she
practicing her digging so one day she could bury Russ? Stop it, I warned
myself—enough with negative thoughts. This was a good thing for both of
them. The truth is Russ and Rose are like silk and steel, and she is not the silk!

I heard them sometimes as doors were slammed and loud words spoken. Nothing really unusual. Couples have their moments, good and bad. I was not basing this on my life which has been empty. I have no experience, only observations. Men never found me attractive and I found them boorish. Women friends, cliques, clubs, volunteer groups were not for me. I am too practical about how I spend my time…couldn't be bothered with stylish clothes or makeup. The only wall mirror I have is a discolored one from a great, great whoever, a grandmother I think, or maybe an aunt. No television. Lots of books whose titles I found on college reading lists.

I am content. I am where I belong. I have retirement money and a meaningless part-time job with people I respect. I've never missed a mortgage payment. I prefer being home and haven't vacationed since my childhood.

I would have stayed cocooned but Rose and Russ broke through my barricade.

I heard them singing as they worked in their garden and laughing as they sat in their rocking chairs on the backyard deck. I joined them every time they invited me and before long, the three of us were together almost every evening. Rose will yada, yada, yada at times filling whatever silence is available. I admired Russ for being patient about this until the day I learned why.

Russ liked to introduce me to the latest additions in his garden as if they were new friends, ones he had always wanted to know. "These are Japanese Painted Ferns. *Athyrium niponicum var pictum* with glimmers of silver and red in the shade. Stunning, don't you think?"

He turned, leading me to another cherished arrival when I asked, "Ever consider teaching a course at the local community college, Russ? Your collections take my breath away, and you are so very knowledgeable."

"One more new plant for you to see," he said.

I touched his arm then said, "Did you hear me, Russ?"

"I did not. Mustn't tell Rose, please. I can't hear very well, don't want hearing aids though. Life is good, Toni," he whispered tilting his head toward

Rose who was carrying a tray of refreshments outside. "Don't want to ruin a good thing. You know what I mean?"

A young couple with three children, all under the age of six, lived in Rose's house. The second winter after their arrival it snowed enough to be measured, almost three inches. They remembered Rose saying to them, "If it ever snows here enough for the children to sleigh ride down the hill, will you invite me to watch? My husband would be delighted, too."

School was canceled that day and Rose called me with such excitement I could hear the smile on her face. She invited me along. I was eager to be part of this fun: I put on my snow boots and with child-like anticipation introduced them to the snow. It fluffed with the lightness of a dry powder each time my foot lifted to advance, then left the prints of my progress following me. I hummed and with each step the faint crunch of the top layer meeting the sogginess of the lower one was proof of my having been there. This snowfall is perfect for sledding. I wanted to be a child again.

We sat bundled on the back porch drinking coffee, hot chocolate, or mulled cider along with homemade biscotti. Russ preferred a sip now and then from his leather flask. He moved his chair closer to Rose, smiled and nudged her. She continued to watch the children. He bent over, rested his head on her shoulder and asked, "Doesn't this have something to do with our finding each other?"

"Only because you were kind and understanding, Russ," she replied never taking her eyes from the snowy hill.

The Rose of days gone by had withered and a new Rose had bloomed before our eyes. The three of us, close friends now, became a team willing to nurture each other. Rose's growth was especially rewarding: she no longer rambled incoherently, she was calm. She learned to listen more and talk less.

Another pleasant outcome of having caring people around her was that she managed to control verbal outbursts most of the time. One day, as Rose sat with me on my front porch, I brought up an issue I didn't think mattered. It did. I had felt it: before seeing it, I knew. She transmitted it to me, or I had become so emotionally attached or I wanted desperately to keep our group together that I became hyper-alert to the tension in her body. I inhaled a deep, slow, breath willing myself to relax. I searched for words to soothe her, hoping to prevent Rose from becoming agitated. I turned toward her and was relieved to see her expression had softened. She paused, looked up to see Russ joining us and announced, "Oh my! Oh my! There's the apple of my eye!" Russ and I shook our heads and laughed: we appreciated this newly discovered technique we labeled *brain interuptus,* a game the three of us would continue to play. When a situation caused her anxiety, we contributed words, phrases, or rhymes to divert Rose's usual responses.

In the ensuing years I softened, became sweet but not sugary. Not a Hallmark movie, but definitely a metamorphosis. I cared and wanted to belong when previously I thought of myself as a loner, usually irritable and impatient with people. Perhaps it was a question of being ready, like a baby hearing songs, rhymes, and stories but unable to repeat them at five weeks old. But given time, and the wonderful repetition of these words, would later echo them over and over again. There is that marvelous occurrence of readiness: similar to my experiencing the pleasure of meaningful friendships. Until the three of us became friends, I preferred isolation because belonging was difficult, relationships end. Feelings get hurt. Saying the right words, fear of being judged made me withdraw into my books. Now, I empathize with their pain and am joyful for their happiness. I feel pride in their accomplish-ments. One can build a wall and feel content until opening the door, entering through it and continuing down a different path. I think I will call it 'growth.'

Years passed. We aged, sooner than expected, and joked at our old people ways. We toasted our glasses of wine, went to bed earlier, did less, ate more, and were filled with sentimental tears when discussing our youth. We hoped it would never end.

It did. Rose died.

CHAPTER 7

Russo and Toni

A WEEK LATER RUSS INVITED ME OVER. ONE ROCKING CHAIR now empty, we sipped our cocktails and sat quietly. The sun moved toward the horizon, the air was humid, and the scent of lilac took up too much space. I poured a fresh drink and relaxed. I waited. The silence was perfect.

He spoke. "I never answered your question the day I gave you the $1,000. I want to tell you now. I'm not sure what motivated me that day I walked into her yard. Something to do with timing maybe. You might not remember, but it was a perfect spring day, exactly like today. All of my senses were heightened. As we retrieved our mail at the curb our eyes met, bringing us close enough for me to sense her energy. I had the impression she nodded to me, as if in greeting. Unusual for her. I crossed the street and followed her as she went to the back yard. I noticed the large hill that came so close to her house.

She was surprised to see me; I had caught her off guard. Realizing my mistake, I was desperate to say something, anything. 'Hill, snow, children… *charge?…*' Whatever came to my mind found its way to my mouth! My words, meant to be fun, bothered her because she had not expected me to be there. I had invaded her space, her privacy. But poison ivy, she was that upset? I knew it was her. Toni, I don't have poison ivy in my yard. I am meticulous about my garden. And, I saw the look in Rose's eyes, the eyes that piqued my interest now scared me as they smoldered with anger. I escaped as quickly as I could. Didn't want to hear whatever she was going to spew. I could not tell you this when I gave you the money for her bail. You would never have consented. We were not close, and even asking you to do this made me uncomfortable. I was relieved when you agreed."

"Why? Tell me why you helped her, Russ. You took a chance asking me. I, like most of the neighbors, preferred the quiet respect for each other and the unspoken rule of never becoming close, revealing too much of a personal nature, and keeping one's distance."

"As the blisters became worse, I became angry at her. I had to do something. My mother used to say, 'Russ, you'll find a solution.' That was her answer for everything. It usually always worked for me whenever I became upset. Toni, I was red-hot, glowing-in-the-dark angry! I needed to know more or get even."

"You are too kind, or you don't know how to get even," I said.

"It was the visceral brooding layer of my soul wanting revenge. Suffering the way I did, the pain and humiliation, the misery all over my body made me decide I would play her game and accept the dinner invitation. I considered being rude, a bad guest in her home, make her miserable during the dinner. One big problem with this plan: these behaviors go against the essence of who I am. Wouldn't, couldn't even attempt to be that kind of person."

Russ looked to the West as the setting sun cast its long shadows across our view. His face had barely aged and the silver in his gray hair captured the life in the sun's rays. He blinked, then turned and looked at me. Had he known I'd been staring at him?

"Rose was wonderful, like no one I had ever known. Her smile, the aroma of pot roast, candles on the table, my flowers, all trimmed and arranged as the centerpiece…this softened my attitude. Rose removing her apron, asking me to uncork the wine, making small talk, feeling welcomed, my pulling out her chair, carving the roast; it all felt so natural, like something we had done many times before. We laughed. We talked and laughed more as we shared childhood memories, teenage angst, and various jobs we tried. She asked so many questions about my life. I would tell her one thing and she would probe and want to know more. Nobody had ever done that before or given me a chance to talk and want to know me. I remember asking myself, 'Is this the same woman who caused me such discomfort?' I discovered feelings I didn't know I had. I learned about myself, Toni, when I heard my own words in expressing feelings and opinions to Rose."

Russ and I moved into the kitchen. We cut cheeses, sliced apples and placed them on a large wooden board with salty crackers, dark bread, meats, and cucumber wedges. We moved about quietly until Russ hummed a song, I recognized it and joined him. I was cleaning knives and small cutting boards at the sink when Russ came behind me and put his hands on my shoulders.

"It's gotten chilly, Toni. Why don't I start a fire and we'll eat in the den?"

We sat on large cushions with a small table between us. The only light was from the fire. Russ continued. "I talked more that evening than in my entire life and it was joyous! She grinned at some of my childhood pranks. When I spoke of sadness in my childhood, she touched my arm, a gesture of sympathy I had never known. She was quiet for a very long time. She listened. When she spoke, she was more perceptive than I could have imagined. We stretched out our hands to each other on the table top, and she rubbed my fingers. We giggled. She looked at me as if I mattered, and I loved her for that. And here I am, thirty years later, with memories of a good marriage to Rose and a lasting friendship with you."

Later, as we cleaned our dishes and wrapped up leftovers, Russ asked if I wanted to move in with him. I declined, at least for now. I preferred my home, my place and my things.

Aging had its way with us over the next three years and we grew more tired; gardened only when necessary so that our plantings languished into old age as well. The fish thrived and I said it was because they could hear the music of Mozart Russ played while we sipped our wine on the deck. We preferred listening rather than talking, relaxing outside on rocking chairs studying the clouds rather than walking. We played Gin Rummy, watched television, remembered Rose, and set a place for her when we ate.

One day, Russ referred to her as Razzle Dazzle Rose.

"Where does that come from?" I asked, recalling her mumbling the words long ago.

"Razzle Dazzle Rose is a name of a crayon and a lipstick. I called her that once. I knew the crayon; she knew the lipstick. I hit a nerve. She turned those dark, beautiful eyes on me and said, 'Never, ever call me that again.' I never did, and I never asked why. Some thoughts are better left unsaid."

My Unholy Trinity

ONCE UPON A TIME I WAS DEAD.

You can see my tombstone on a hill between a chain-link fence and the cemetery road that, on a curve, runs too close to my casket and thus causes much panic within me for fear of losing my toes, or, at least, the bones of them. I have lost so much already.

I was buried here, and not out of love, along the property line of the Cemetery of a Joyful After Life when farms and forests surrounded it. Shortly after my interment, row houses were constructed near me. Families were moving out of the city and into my peacefulness. For decades I have heard their lives unravel as they serve up their dinners, water their gardens, or yell at their kids. They argue and pester each other and place trash cans in the alleys which are quite close to my plot, too close on a hot day when men run late with their trucks and the air becomes putrid, like me.

In 1912, when I was fifteen and living with my family in Sicily, my brother, Antony, came to me as I was cooking breakfast. He said he was taking his wife, Santina, and going to America. This place offered him nothing, he told me. He wanted more. "I have decided, Matiana, that it is good for you to join us. Mama has Leo and Marianna now to help her."

How kind and thoughtful this new beginning sounded.

I paused. Antony gasped, probably expecting I would quickly agree with him. Believe me when I tell you I was content with my circumstances. The people here are good natured, and the wine inspires them to sing and dance. Sicily is famous for its vineyards: the stories of times long ago hold their attention, some with sentimental yearning. The food is bold with spices and herbs, rich in flavor, and shared with neighbors who are enticed by an aroma riding the pleasant breezes.

Antony awaited my answer, but before I could say anything, he hugged me and said, "We leave tomorrow, Matiana. Sense the adventure of going to America with us!"

And so it was. We packed our trunks, parted with tears and hugs, kisses, and blessings, then sailed west with plans, hopes, and dreams.

Antony was true to his word and our lives took on a pleasant routine in a small basement apartment. We had jobs, shared household duties, and contributed to a general expense fund. For three years we lived in harmony until I met Pietro. Oh, such love, such sweetness. He smiled deeply and his full cheeks created lines an artist's pencil would envy. We walked hand in hand through the park. He whistled, tilted his head to model a white summer straw hat, his latest purchase. He turned and walked backwards singing "O Solo Mio". Then swiping his hat from his head, he bowed low before me and apologized for being off key. Such fun and laughter was my Pietro.

Last week his dark eyes looked down into mine. As always, he grinned and I wondered would he be funny, dramatic, or serious? There were many different Pietros. He placed his thumbs through his suspenders and excitedly announced a new idea, a plan for making money, becoming rich he said, like Americans. He called it the stock market and he could invest, earn money without working! I was awestruck and would tell Antony about this market. I wished him luck getting rich and wanted to hug him. As I drew near, he pulled back and shook my hand like I have seen men do.

On my eighteenth birthday, Antony wanted to celebrate. I was a young woman now, he had announced proudly. He was going to take us to dinner, to the fancy restaurant two blocks away in the shopping district.

"We have a present for you, sister," he said while Santina handed me a flowered box that was trimmed with wide, red ribbon. My eyes teared with surprise. I pulled the ribbon's end and lifting the lid saw a sheer layer of delicate cloth covering a white dress with long sleeves and delicate pearl buttons at the cuffs. The narrow black belt would emphasize my small waist.

As I dressed for dinner I chose to use the red ribbon in place of the belt. I looped a bow at the front then carefully slid the shiny ribbon to the back of the dress. I pictured the two long hanging ends flitting about, marking each step with its elegance.

"Where's the belt, Matiana?" Antony asked with a sullen pout.

I looked down, moved my fingers along the ribbon's edge. I began to stutter a response when Santina interrupted.

"Antony, I am ready. Stop fussing and let us leave now," she said with a wink in my direction.

"He does not always understand us, does he? Old country attitude he brings with him," she whispered to me as Antony locked the door.

He seemed taller as he walked between us with arms hooked. He looked to see if neighbors noticed our passing as they chatted and sat on folding chairs or white marble steps. Whether they did or did not, Antony announced how lucky he was to have two dark-haired beauties on each arm, saying, "Bella ragazza, bella ragazza."

As we approached the restaurant, I saw Pietro across the street. He winked. His friends began to tease and prod him. I lifted my head higher. A girl in tight jeans took his hand, then glared at me over large framed sunglasses.

Antony looked at me, then to Pietro. I felt his arm tighten. He stared in Pietro's direction, then pulled me closer.

Later that week, Antony informed me that he had made a decision. Back in the day, it was the man of the house, a father or a brother, who determined the futures of daughters, sisters and mothers. "And wives," Santina would have added.

"It is time, Matiana, for you to marry."

I nodded in agreement, imagining Pietro and me together. But he had not yet been properly introduced to Antony. They had never spoken.

"I have sent for Francesco."

He means Pietro. He must mean Pietro, I thought.

"You recall Francesco? A good boy. Hard worker. Honest and caring. He has helped Mama many times since we have gone. He is good for you, Matiana. He will love you, and you will have many beautiful babies."

"I love Pietro. It is he I will marry!"

"Pietro is not good for you. It will be Francesco and this is my final word."

"You can't do this to me! I don't love him! Pietro and I love each other!"

Then pointing my finger at him, I spoke without thinking. "I remember your pathetic words the day you brought Santina to dinner to tell us of your engagement. Holding your wine glass high, you had proudly stated, 'Every foot needs a shoe that fits, and Santina is my shoe'. What clumsy words, Antony! You should hear the poetic words of Pietro; his delicious sounds are music, tugging at my soul, my heart! 'Amore,' he whispers, words of love."

"Matiana! Stop! It is done. You will learn to love Francesco. It is what wives must do. That, and make families."

Pietro betrayed me. He would not elope, even though I begged him with tears in my eyes. I beseeched him to sleep with me and make a baby so my family would disown me—a sure way to prevent a marriage to one I did not love! He laughed.

"Am I Antony's property, like his car? How can my brother do this, Pietro? This is America and I am owned by the customs of a foreign country I will never see again! Why won't you help me? Do you no longer love me?"

"I must do what your brother says, Matiana, or I will be an outcast. My family, this neighborhood, would spit at the mention of my name," Pietro said without emotion. For him, this was easy. He had choices. He was the only son in a family of four sisters.

My clenched hands reached toward his chest but he was faster and grabbed my wrists, twisted them outward. My knees buckled as I cried out in pain. Letting them go, Pietro turned away, whistled, and tipped his hat to neighbors who had gathered at their front doors. "The show is over," I yelled as they retreated back to their dinners.

I loathed my life with Francesco. We had five children. Their dark eyes, thick black hair, and beautiful skin depressed me. They resembled Francesco or his family. He was a good father and husband which caused me more misery. I could not hate him but I would never love him.

Nothing warmed my heart. And always I imagined the life I might have had with Pietro who promised me so much, who said we would marry when he could afford a house. Pietro, who charmed me. He spoke words laced with romance and dreams, then abandoned me so easily, reminding me to obey my brother. I cursed his name every night after I said my rosary.

Francesco and Antony were friends, 'pisans' they said. Our rowhouses were next to each other in an Italian neighborhood. The yards were small so Francesco and Antony removed the fence between them making a space for a large swimming pool. The water splashed all day with shouts of Marco Polo. Santina's children fought with ours and voices would grow louder. The men ignored this and waited for them to get quiet, then screamed when they did not. This happened many times. Children yelled at each other: fathers yelled at children. A few minutes of peace then the cycle continued.

I had been asked to make ice tea for the husbands as they sat in folding chairs on our small, concrete space. Patio, they called it. I disagreed. It was ugly concrete. I waited for the water to boil. Santina was napping. How could she sleep with this shouting? I think she took pills.

I fixed a tray while finding fault with everything around me in a small, cluttered kitchen where I was expected to cook three meals a day. Francesco, always smiling, would kiss me on my neck while sauce bubbled all over the range that he did not have to clean. I daydreamed a different life and he did not know. Why did he not? Because I smiled too. I acted the part I had been given. As I did now, opening the door, serving the tea, being thanked and asked to join them as one lights up his cigar. A child jumped in the pool: shrill shouts followed. I dropped a glass and Francesco noted goodheartedly, "Good thing that it is aluminum one, yes, Matiana? Nothing to clean up."

I was a soldier fighting to survive. My enemies have control. I offered an appreciative glance in their direction. Yet, my deception weighed upon me. I searched for someone or something to cherish. The neighbors said, *fortunate*, when they compared their husbands to Francesco. I used to nod in agreement. I practiced every day to hide my ugly true self.

I did not belong here. But every minute I pretended I did.

Approaching our 25th wedding anniversary, doctors confirmed that Francesco had an inoperable tumor. He would die within a year.

Did I say to myself, "Finally, I am free? " Would you think me wicked?

Antony wanted to speak to me, alone. We went for a walk. He said he had made a decision. Not again I moaned to my inside screaming self.

He had purchased four grave sites. I weakened.

He held my arm. My breath was gone. The world had stopped. What happened to the sun? To the bird song?

I tried to hear his words. Could not, and wanted this nightmare to end.

His face came close, large hands grabbed my shoulders and worried eyes mourned the loss of his friend then quickly danced awake with the thought of his grand gesture. "A gift for all eternity," I think he might have said. "The four of us who loved each other and have been so devoted will be together here under magnificent oak trees," he bragged while unfolding a pamphlet. "Our headstones are large with angels adorning each side, reaching their arms upward. It is magnificent, Matiana!"

He said 'devoted.' I have been the best actress on this stage.

I waited until two days after Francesco was buried. I said to my brother, "We need to talk. *I have made a decision.*"

We sat at his kitchen table. I poured two whiskeys over ice.

"Drink, Antony, for you will need it. Now look at me. See my eyes. Hear these words: I will never, ever lay next to you or Francesco for eternity."

He gulped his drink and poured another and tried to interrupt me.

"Listen to me, Antony. Say nothing and hear my words! If I die before you, and I welcome its release from a life not of my choosing, do what I say or I will curse you until the day you die and forever after. I will curse Santina and your children and your children's children. But I will curse you first and strongest every day. I have lived a lie and I will not continue this into death. It does not matter where in the cemetery you choose to bury me, as long as it is as far away as possible from you and Francesco. Neither rest nor peace would I find with another of your selfish, old country ideas. Large oak trees? How beautiful you make it sound. You have had your dreams and they have been my nightmares! I have suffocated myself with anger for too long and I will call upon it in my dying to punish you."

We lived side by side for several more years, keeping our secret. I reminded him from time to time about the curse. He responded with silence and a wrinkled brow.

One day he was combing his hair while looking into a mirror.

"Lest you forget, Antony," I said with my hand on his shoulder, both of us seeing our shared reflection. "You will find me some place else to be. I don't care where, just not next to your friend, Francesco."

"Your husband, too, sister."

"Chosen by you, brother."

And with that I nudged him hard. His comb dropped and I kicked it the length of the hall where family portraits hung. It stopped under my wedding picture. Antony shivered. I grinned. I sensed victory.

Remembering now, feeling the bitterness in my rotting corpse, I wonder if I should have made this effort to speak to you. Does it ease my burden? I fear it does not. If only I knew how my life would unfold; how my wishes, no, more than that, my happiness would be ignored, betrayed in the name of duty to others, I would never have left home where the land and its people welcomed each day with the joy of being alive.

I ache and curse the three men whose names I will not say—the brother, the lover, the other …. my unholy trinity.

Loreli

CHAPTER 1

Together Again

I HAD ENTERED A RELIC: THE DEEP-DOWN, DIRTY DARKNESS of a bar on a lonely Virginia country road with just enough colored neon to blur the sense of time. I sat at a table where four men were sharing a bottle of Jack. They ignored me and went about the business of team scores and complaints about their women. I turned my chair around until my eyes had an unobstructed view of the door. The bartender grinned while he wiped down the long wooden bar.

I had plenty of time to watch and wait. I'm patient when I have to be and started my second bottle of Natty Boh. Loyalty to Baltimore made this my beer of choice. Would this be the day I had been planning on for so long? Every time a slash of daylight pierced the darkness, I looked to see if it would be her.

And Natty Boh number four was the lucky one!

I grinned at her large, full, pointed breasts, Playtex 38D, circa 1951. They pulled her torso forward and down as she maneuvered herself toward the bar in red stiletto heels. Talking, drinking and dart throwing ceased. In unison, all heads followed her movement, which was slow, deliberate. Her lips smiled coyly. She glanced to her right as if making sure she was the object of their attention.

How could she have thought otherwise? I wondered.

Her sheer, blue blouse did nothing to camouflage the objects of their desire. Ruffles fell over the cantilevered shelf of her bosom and came to an abrupt end at a belted waist that seemed to hold together the torso and bottom part of her body. The tight black skirt cooperated as it clung to her ass and thighs. I marveled at the elegant taper of her legs and the delicate, small ankle balancing in the high heels.

How do they hold her up? I mused.

"The same way a thoroughbred functions," came a snickered retort from behind me.

Had I spoken aloud?

A hush filled the room as she leaned over the bar, scanning the labels. Every man raised from his chair, peering into the mirror and hoping to spy reflected cleavage. I sat.

I had searched for months, worried about her, made a promise to help her, had been staking out Larry's bar knowing one day she would walk through the door and today she did!

"Grey Goose on the rocks, Larry," she spoke in a southern-trying-too-hard accent. Her audience approved her choice, I suppose, because heads were bobbing up and down in unison. Hips shifted. Black, wavy, shoulder-length hair was tossed with a well-practiced move of the head. Red fingernails reached for the iced vodka.

"On the house, Sal," Larry said with a wink.

He knows her as Sal. She's been in here before. She raised her glass to him, and then turned to observe the onlookers. In an awkward instant, her glass slipped to the floor and shattered. Clear liquid and stiletto heel met at the same moment. A collective gasp and Sal's scream occurred simultaneously as she fell to the floor. The spandex skirt pulled tightly around her thighs as she hit bottom sitting with both legs straight out in front. She assessed where she was and what had happened, then raised her head, looked around the room and chuckled.

"Is this for real, or what?" asked the voice behind me.

Everyone else was in motion. The heroes restored dignity to the woman I know as Loreli. With careful engineering, they managed to position her quickly into an upright position. This monument to womanhood smiled, brushed at her blouse, and thanked them.

Moving as one, Sal, accompanied by her drones, sought a comfortable chair. Larry followed the awkward procession with a refill.

She stopped her entourage, our eyes met, and she said, "Hello, Pops. How's tricks?"

"I might ask you the same question."

She directed her subjects to pull out the chair. *This is going to be fun*, I thought. I watched her as she watched me. Let the games begin.

CHAPTER 2

My Gal Sal? Not Really!

I WALKED INTO HER NO-FRILLS APARTMENT, UNLOCKING THE door with the key she slipped to me at the bar. She was clever, always wanting to test everyone's ability to match her wit. I listened closely as she worked her address into the conversation. She knew I would know. We have a history.

Her place was minimalistic, monastic, boring. Also clean and relaxing with a nod toward caring attested to by the presence of a large-leafed plant whose branches reached across the space where a couch might be. I checked for beer. None. I checked for crackers and cheese. Nothing. Not the same person I remembered.

An hour later, she opened the door, smiled, and I followed her to the bedroom where she began to undress.

"Make yourself comfortable. Enjoy."

"I'm trying to, *Sal*," I laughed. "But it's a bit difficult with no refreshments. I'm guessing this is not your place. Doesn't suit either Sal or Loreli!" I said.

"You do know me, Dan. I'm house sitting for a friend, a connection who's helped me before. He's ascetic, solitary, doesn't talk much. In other words, he's perfect for this job. I should have been smarter and involved you in my search," she admitted while pulling off the wig then a tight constricting cap. She ran her fingers through her dark, very short hair and sighed.

"It's taken a long time, don't you agree? My Plan A was disastrous. Plan B was too risky. I'd be embarrassed to tell you how I failed. Thought this would take a couple of weeks, didn't you? Who knew Larry could be clever? But here we are, the two of us, and we found him," she said while coming closer to me.

I smiled and pulled her to me. I had been missing Lo for a very long time. She drew back and grabbed the two sides of her blue blouse, yanked them apart, ripping the fabric and sending buttons arcing across the room.

"Ruffles, I can't stand them!"

She yanked and tugged, she damned her articles of bondage as each piece was tossed up, over, and around the room. The overstuffed padded bra was tossed my way, hit me in the face, and fell to my feet.

"Here. men are obsessed with what these hold. You wear it! Go on, I dare you," she giggled.

I did. I placed it on my head, cups pointed up and began to sing M-I-C-K-E-Y M-O-U-S E!

"Well, now you've ruined one of my favorite old, black-and-white TV shows! I wanted to be Annette Funicello!"

We laughed as she continued to shed the outer shell of Sal.

I enjoyed the transformation to the girl I call Lo. On her bed lay the usual black tee shirt and jeans. Expensive leather ankle boots were nearby.

"Let's talk after I shower and while we eat sushi."

We were presented with selections of salmon, ahi tuna, cold saki, and two cold beers. It's what we do—toast with saki, then beer with the sushi. Chopsticks, soy sauce, and ginger were placed on the table. We ate slowly, savoring each morsel.

"I'd been expecting you. I knew you would help me."

"I knew that you knew that! I have one question. The red stiletto heels, really? And the fall … it took every bit of control not to laugh out loud! Didn't I teach you better than that?"

"You taught me how to count. You just asked two questions."

We tapped our beer bottles with the good feeling I always had when we were together.

"Bad choice, using those stiletto heels. But I did practice. What I could not account for, however, was my shock in seeing your face reflected in the mirror behind the bar. I reacted, turned too quickly and there you were, grinning and looking foolish!"

"That makes two of us," I responded.

"Dan, what a disguise! I like the mustache. But not that much. Get rid of it, please. The pillow-in-the pants part of your getup was too weird, not funny. I would have thought an ex-policeman would do better with undercover assignments!"

"Not fair," I pouted. "I was on foot patrol and new to the job."

"Comical, Mr. Pillow Pants. Were you trying to keep *me* from seeing you too? We're together now and we can get Busha's ring from that miserable, lying, cheating…" and her voice trailed off as she stabbed a piece of sushi.

I said, "I found Larry when I mangled his Mustang two weeks ago. Lo, I knew you would show up, sooner or later. I've been stopping in at different times, three days a week. Most amusing time I ever had was earlier today. What a show! Quite the crowd pleaser, aren't you? I was just another smiling face."

CHAPTER 3

In The Beginning

LO'S GRANDMOTHER IS CECYLIA NOWAK. EVERYONE CALLS her Busha, the Polish word meaning grandmother. This suits her as she is considered by many to be the town's matriarch. Nowak, pronounced Novak, means "new one" as in the new person in town. It can also mean novice or stranger. Her Polish friends interpret the word to mean pioneer which they feel describes her best. I came to know how she fulfilled this role. Indeed, Busha was a very busy pioneer. For twenty-five years, she has owned and operated a small grocery store specializing in all things Polish. Her customers came through Ellis Island about the same time as the Nowak's and most continued to speak Polish when shopping there. Busha honored purchases on credit and marked accounts in a black and white marbleized copybook—the same kind the children used in school. Customers paid when they could and usually in a timely fashion. Busha knew when their money was low because they stopped coming to the store. Looking after her community, Busha would leave a bag of food by their door. Prices were reduced and marked 'on sale'. She never recorded these in the account book.

Busha took pleasure in lending money to those in need. She could be ruthless in selecting the recipients, judging each person's merit or circumstance according to the purpose for the loan. Wanting to pay off a gambling debt? Thumbs down means the same thing in most cultures.

Every Sunday she wore a black-laced mantilla on her head, genuflected in St. Stanislaus Church with a wink and a grin to Father Rolanski, then slid herself across the pew while former clients paid the deference she was due with whispers of respect.

I once owed Busha $100.00. My marriage was sliding sideways. My "starter wife" was making my life miserable, spending money I hadn't earned, refusing to get a job, and nagging me to ask for a raise. Clearly, she did not understand the salary regulations of a Baltimore City policeman walking patrol on the rough side of town. And, yes, I did try explaining this to her and wondered each time she looked at me with her empty eyes surrounded by black caked-on mascara, *Why the hell I married her!*

"Hey, starter wife!" I yelled one night after a grueling night on the streets. "Can you at least have a meal for me once in a while?"

She was at the door, ready to meet her friends at the local bar.

"What did you call me, Dan?"

"Starter wife! As in the next one will be THE one, the good wife!"

Next day, she was gone. So was everything of any value. I opened the door after completing a day shift, and our miserable looking apartment was empty. It never looked better. She wasn't in it! But neither was my collection of baseball cards. Damn! My closet was empty. I followed a noxious smell and found my clothes in the bathtub with bleach. Double Damn! The beer was gone, too. I really wanted a drink. And I needed money.

That is how I came to know Busha. I had heard her name passed around the station from time to time, never really paying close attention until now.

I took the number 27 bus. Rain poured the minute the door opened and I walked the ten blocks to Midtown Grocery wearing my uniform—a serious breach of protocol since I was off duty.

I entered a clean, well-organized store—canned goods neatly arranged on white shelves, fresh produce in arrays of color along a wall and cuts of meats in the cases with reasonable pricing. The skies cleared and clean windows allowed the setting sun to paint the aisles, cases, and produce in a mellow, pastel light.

Standing near the register, an ebony skinned man was handing a wad of cash to a short woman wearing a long, flowery cotton dress. Her gray hair in a single braid ended at the ties of her white apron. He was smiling, looking grateful. He was clothed in bright colors, fabric of yellow and brown swirls, symbols I did not know. He stood erect, squared shoulders, seeming proud and of noble bearing. As he turned to leave, a young woman moved into his spot. The same money was then placed in her open palm with Polish words spoken between the smiling women.

Busha turned to me saying, "Why you leak water on my scrubbed floor?"

I stammered, explained how a buddy recommended her, told her I needed help.

Bold eyes narrowed as she examined me in my dark blue and very wet uniform. I was ashamed. I removed my hat, held it in front of me, looked into her eyes, and asked to borrow $100.00. She asked no questions and gave me $135.00.

"You look like shit. You only pay back $100.00. I do you this favor," she said.

"Come back to kitchen. Dinner is almost done. I feed you just this once."

She pulled aside a narrow curtain. The aroma of beef, potatoes, and apple pie filled a very large living space and would ease the pain in my very empty stomach.

'Just this once' turned into my living in Busha's basement and eating meals which were served on a regular basis. In return, I did her bidding when not on duty.

"Pretend I am Robinson Crusoe. You are my Saturday," she had said.

"You mean Friday."

"What? What happens Friday? Do we have plan or something?"

"Busha! No plan. I would be your Friday"

"There you do it again, Dan! You would be here Friday? What is meaning?"

Busha had a list that included tasks requiring skills in home repairs, all of which I am lacking. I felt as though I was outside looking in and seeing a bad ending of a very good thing. So I lied.

"Sure, I can replace those two windows and lay tile in the bathroom."

So I became her Saturday. And I learned from books, do-it-yourself magazines, and assistance from Jim of J&P'S Hardware & Bar. Hardware store out front with an antique John Deere tractor in the large display window and a no-nonsense bar in the back operated by his daughter Patricia, or as the older Polish patrons called her, Patritsya.

I was in the hardware store for my first lesson in Carpentry 101. Jim led me down the aisles, stopping at a small tools area. He talked, I asked questions and took notes. He left to help a customer at the register and I browsed and priced wrenches and screwdrivers. I liked being here; I felt I belonged. The creaking wooden floor was old and I could feel the warmth of generations of carpenters' boots with each step. The aroma of Jim's newly arrived shipment of lumber outside in the yard found its way to me at aisle five. I stopped, jangled through the nuts and bolts and smiled. My daydream of becoming a master carpenter shattered at the sound of a high-pitched key-cutting machine. I paid Jim, thanked him for his help and left for home. It is *my home*, isn't it?

As I turned the corner, I saw Busha sitting on the wooden bench out side her store. She was dozing and I was reminded of yesterday when Busha mentioned I would soon meet Lo. She smiled. Then turned serious as she told be her granddaughter was worried about her forgetting things, making mistakes, growing old. "She watches me like greyhound."

"Hawk, you mean hawk ... as in 'watches me like a hawk.' "

"Whatever, she does it. Check to see stove is off or if I remember to pay bills, or count right change from register. This makes me crazy, but will work it out; we always do."

Before I met Lo, I heard her voice. I was cleaning up the dust after installing a new doorknob for the bathroom, one that could now be locked rather than the old-fashioned hook and eye. The two women whispered in the store and the curtain did little to muffle their voices. I could tell they loved each other: their voices softened and words were spoken in a tone one saves for people they respect.

"Busha, why? I don't understand. He's a stranger. How do we know we can trust him?"

Their tender voices grew louder, each becoming impatient with the other's opinion concerning me. I hesitated, wondering what to do. But only briefly. It's not in my nature to ponder. Instinctively, I went through into the store. Their heads turned. I looked at Lo, whose wide, dark eyes turned icy. Long legs, longer strides, and a pointed finger nearing my face, but not for long, because I turned, went to the kitchen, opened a beer, and sat down at the table. No one is ever allowed to point a finger at me. That is rule number one.

I expected Lo and Busha to follow. Wrong. Two unpredictable women talked in a mixture of English and Polish. I mulled over my future. Fifteen minutes later, Lo came into the kitchen, opened a beer, and sat at the table with me.

"Busha likes you, really likes you. She's always been a good judge of character. I respect her feelings."

She took a few gulps of beer. I wasn't expecting her to sip it. She studied my face. I let her and tilted my head a bit so she might take into account my strong jaw line. It was my best feature a girlfriend once said as she traced along it with her finger. But Lo's eyes were moving over the gray hair around my temple. These were a recent development. I hoped they made me look distinguished. At thirty-four, I was taking after my dad.

"Here's what's going to happen. You can live here until there's a reason for you not to. You seem like one of the good guys. You have made a difference here while I was away. I like that. Busha, my dear Busha, has become more vulnerable, sometimes forgets things. She appeals to most people with her silver hair, floral frocks, and calm demeanor. Busha is everybody's grand-mother. I can't believe I said *frocks!* Bottom line: she belongs to me, but I will share Busha with you as long you respect her. In other words, no flirting."

"WHAT?!" I yelled as beer splattered from my mouth.

"Good response," she laughed, winked, and tapped her bottle to mine.

After coffee and eggs the next morning, Lo said, "Busha asked me to take you out back to the shed. No, Dan, you're not in trouble, well not yet, but who knows what the future holds," she said with a smile. In an old shed behind the house, she introduced me to her grandfather's tools, naming each one, handling them with respect for the hands that once held them. The smell of old wood chips held the history of a talented man building functional proj-ects for his family and neighbors. We were finished, ready to leave, when Lo paused, then turned to look back into the shed. I sensed flashes of sentimental remembrances from her childhood.

CHAPTER 4

The Neighborhood

THE POLISH NEIGHBORHOOD WAS CLEAN AND PEACEFUL
with moderate to low-income housing. Residents ranged from toddlers to
retired people who would remain there until they could no longer. People
walked to stores, churches, a nearby clinic, and a small park with lush grass,
wild flowers and sky-reaching oak trees.

Father Rolanski was born into this neighborhood seventy-three years
ago and assigned there shortly after his ordination because he spoke Polish
and English. Years ago, when he first arrived, he needed $400.00 to pay for
kitchen repairs in the old rectory after the diocese refused due to lack of
funds. He earned very little and his family was poor. A bargain was made with
Busha who would forgo her weekly envelope contribution until his debt was
repaid. In this respect, she was a businesswoman who realized there must be
no exceptions in her system, not even for the parish priest.

So gentle was his voice during sermons that devoted parishioners tried,
with some success, to read his lips. A concentrated silence throughout the
small stone church, with adults leaning forward to draw closer to him,
resulted in a spiritual atmosphere. They loved their kind priest and invited
him to Sunday dinners where he would bless the food, then eat little of it.
When prodded, Father would sing the Polish songs from his childhood, but
softly, ever so softly.

A few days ago, Busha 'donated' money to Father Rolanski to replace the rotting steps of the rectory. Donated money, I learned, was given, not to be repaid. He had not petitioned the diocese for the funds because he felt it was his responsibility. That, and the good Father did not want to draw attention to himself lest they replace him because of his age.

"After all," he mumbled, "I've lived in the rectory for fifty-five years. The steps are old and splintered much like me. It's the least I can do."

Replacing wooden steps with concrete ones created lots of excitement and a steady request for them was keeping me busy. Elderly sidewalk super-intendents pulled up chairs and became my audience. Kindly, they plied me with iced tea or hot coffee, depending on the weather. They offered sugges-tions, went to the hardware store when I asked, talked politics and sports, and sometimes dozed. Business was good and I was considering going full time and quitting the force.

Saturday's jobs also included money deliveries. It started when Busha asked me to take a food order and a 'donation' to her friend Kazia who, when I arrived, invited me in for a cup of coffee. I sensed loneliness and her need for company so I stayed and listened.

As Kazia poured the coffee, Lo entered. She kissed Kazia's forehead then poured herself a cup.

"Kazia's coffee is the best, the strongest coffee ever. She percolates it all day so by 4 o'clock one gets used to it."

Kazia laughed, "She says 'one' gets used to it. The one is me, usually by myself! Except for you, Lo. You take me for haircut and visit and chat over coffee. Thank you."

I had forgotten about the wad of cash, pulled it from my jacket, and slid it across the table to Kazia who seemed embarrassed, but thanked me.

"Busha is so good to us," she sighed.

"Busha," Lo said, "can afford to be good to people like you. It pleases her. It's why she's always happy."

She placed her hand over Kazia's. We sipped our coffee while Kazia told us about her arthritis medications. Between sips, Lo and I smiled across the table, occasionally contributing sympathetic comments.

When we said our good-byes, I asked, "Can Busha afford to do this? Her store earns, but certainly not enough for the loans." Then realizing how I sounded added, "Sorry, I didn't mean to pry."

"Sure you did. And, yes, she can. I have to get ready. I'm meeting Larry in 45 minutes."

It was the first time I had heard his name.

"Larry?" Did I sound possessive, jealous? Hell, yes!

But she was four strides ahead of me and quickly disappeared into Busha's shop.

CHAPTER 5

Larry

———

THAT NIGHT, I STAYED IN THE KITCHEN WAITING FOR LO TO return. She didn't.

Hours later, I fixed breakfast for Busha. I couldn't eat.

"Lo must be really tired today," she observed while swirling toast through the once-over-easy egg. "Usually the smell of coffee is like rooster. I think it is alarm clock. No?"

"Yes," I replied as she handed me a list of odd jobs. I loaded my truck and headed for Kazia's house. She answered the door wearing a powder-blue chenille robe and two rollers in her hair which were working their way down her forehead. I smiled, stepped inside as she removed the rollers, and we walked back to her kitchen.

"Who is Larry?" I asked.

"He is snake."

"Not telling me enough, but you do have me worried."

The cup was in her hand, but I said no to the strongest coffee ever and sat down.

"He is viper. But one in sheep's clothing."

Our heads turned as the stairs creaked, a moan, another step with a grunt, and Lo limped into the kitchen toward me. I stood and she leaned into me. It felt so natural. As I raised my arm towards her shoulder, she pulled away. Her denim jacket was torn. A bruise was forming on her cheek; there was a cut on her forehead.

"What happened? Did Larry do this? Who is he? No, where is he?" I asked.

"He's in the emergency room, I think, maybe, I hope so. If you think I look bad, you ought to see him. I was afraid to go home, didn't want to upset Busha. Help me, Dan. Could you distract Busha by asking her about the shed repairs? If you are out back, I can get to my room. And, Kazia, thanks for letting me stay the night."

We left, hurrying the few blocks to Busha's place without speaking. How strong was Lo if Larry was in the ER?

Bad news: She had used a baseball bat.

More bad news: They were married.

News gets better: Marriage wasn't legal.

Bad again: Both were intoxicated, couldn't respond, and passed out.

Strange news: An unofficial marriage certificate was rolled and stuffed into Larry's trousers where his wallet used to be.

Good news: The so-called minister and witness were in jail.

Question: Do I want to get involved with Lo?

Answer: Definitely!

We planned to meet and talk tomorrow about the events of the last twenty-four hours.

CHAPTER 6

Our Picnic

THE NEXT DAY, PATRICIA PACKED A PICNIC FOR LO AND ME.
She needed some floor work done and bar shelves braced. She took care
of her elderly mother: money was tight. I do what locals call "courtesy," as
in "I can do you the courtesy of supplying you with a lunch in return for
your helping me." Hard to resist a small cooler of beer, she now carried
Natty Boh for me, and her homemade potato salad along with corn beef
sandwiches.

The picnic basket rested between me and Lo. The beer was in the bed of
my truck. The ride was silent—an uncomfortable, tense silence. I turned on
a country music station. She turned it off. I fussed with the rear-view mirror.
She looked out the side window.

I pulled into a grassy area with trees and three wooden tables. Lo put
the food on a checkered tablecloth and we sat on benches facing each other.
With lowered head, she placed her hands, with no bracelets or rings, over her
face. Would tears be next? If so, what would I do? How well do I know her?

Her fingers parted and revealed teasing eyes. She laughed and whispered, "Peek-a-boo! No need to worry about me. I'm a big girl, and I can take
care of myself. Or others, if need be."

"Others meaning Larry?"

She chuckled, approved of the light-hearted atmosphere, unwrapped
sandwiches while I served the potato salad and opened the beers.

"Larry has…," she hesitated. Her mood became serious, melancholy even as she continued. "Larry has stolen Busha's ring. How could he do this to her? To me? Dan, this ring is exceptional. It is carved from a single piece of black onyx, believed by ancient cultures in her region of Poland to be a powerful protective stone. It has been handed down from one grandmother to another because the people felt it provided emotional and physical strength."

The sky darkened as we bit into our sandwiches. I hadn't realized how hungry I was.

"What region, Lo? How serious are you about the stone's protective power? Do you believe it?"

She finished eating, wiped her mouth, and answered me.

"My people originated from a small village. The closest city, but still quite far away, is Bogdanka. The coal mine there is one of the most profitable in all of Poland. Some of the people have old ways, customs, and superstitions and believe this ring is a catalyst for improving their lives. The ring does nothing, but their belief is so strong that even when events do not improve, they find good reasons why. Then accept or change what they can. Like her loans, Busha passes the ring to those who request it because they are struggling, physically or emotionally. She has no secret words, no incantations, just the polished black onyx with an inlaid pattern of an arrow. It is meant to be worn at night while sleeping or placed under one's pillow. It must only be used at night for the blackness of the ring and the darkness of the sky are symbolic."

"The ring is the reason for your bruises? Did you fight with Larry?" I interrupted.

I was finishing my lunch and, as if to assist her in evading the subject, winds whipped wildly around us. A sudden heavy rain pounded us and we gathered what we could, dashed to the truck and laughed like the children we used to be.

I love her sense of humor in all things ordinary or not. She adapts and laughs at herself or the situation. She carries me along with her in the fun of the moment. She didn't worry about getting drenched like other women I have known: the dramatic-damsels-in-distress kind that whine and worry that their hair is getting wet, that run for cover without lending a hand to clean up after a picnic, that can be unpredictable, laughing one minute and complaining the next. A man's attempt to soothe with, I'll get the truck...or the umbrella...or here, take my jacket...or maybe, 'Sorry Hon, I should have checked the weather'... will not matter. Don't get me wrong. I have been a gentleman many times: I relish it, especially when I care deeply for someone. And I was beginning to feel that way about Lo.

As I pulled onto the road, she kissed my cheek and said, "We passed a diner on the way. Let's stop in for coffee and pie. I must tell you about Larry's miserable attempt to marry me. If only he knew me better; if only I had realized his silly obsession."

Raindrops raced to the bottom of the large window that overlooked the empty parking lot. The coffee was hot, the pie was warm and the melting ice cream on top created modern art for my fork.

She told me they dated in high school. She ended it when he got involved with a gang that enjoyed drinking, racing cars down the main street, playing music too loud and too late and pestering anyone who called the police. He grew up, eventually, but not enough to gain the respect of the community.

"Over the years, every now and then, he calls. We see each other for dinner and talk. I try to help him sort out his issues. He tells me he tries to control his rage. I don't think he is ever happy, always some chip on his shoulder about being misunderstood. You've known people like him: it's never Larry's fault. The marriage I don't remember, he doesn't either, but says he does. Insists it was legal. I remember being dizzy, confused, and fighting with him. It seemed like hours, not days, of being missing. I slept and woke up in his Mustang that was parked outside of his apartment. I got out and stood in the drizzle because it felt good. Anger and pain propelled me two floors up to his apartment as I recalled a motel room and the two of us fighting. I pounded on his door, he opened it, and I saw him wearing Busha's ring. That's when I punched him!"

She lowered her head, leaned in close, and seethed through clenched teeth, "He was not wearing it when he picked me up for dinner. A lot must have happened in the hours I could not remember. I guessed Larry had drugged me. I worried what else he may have done. What scum, don't you agree?"

I nodded. She continued. Her voice grew louder and her cheeks colored. "I grabbed a baseball bat that was leaning against the door frame. I was afraid of him: had he hurt Busha?"

I am hearing lawyer speak, *"Intent to do bodily harm."*

"You aren't going anywhere, are you, Larry?" I asked him as I pointed the bat at two suitcases. He was rubbing his jaw and looked dazed."

" 'What the hell, Lo?' He said while regaining his balance."

"Dan, I tried to settle myself, but the ring, his mother, and the suitcases—I worried he would hurt me."

"His mother?" I asked. "What has she got to do with this?"

Silence. She looked at the movement of the rain on the window. I followed her gaze. Lo's reflection was covered with raindrops, like tears, falling outside, the other side, and washing over her on the inside.

"Lo?" I whispered.

"Yesterday, he pawned his mother's wheelchair while she was still in it. I planned on asking him about this during dinner. Onlookers said he was laughing while his mother appeared frightened. The clerk asked about his mother but he smirked, offered no explanation, then carried her out of the shop, put her in his Mustang and made a real show of screeching tires as he sped away."

She took a deep breath and placed her hands over mine. Her eyes closed. "Just Walking in the Rain" played from the jukebox. Lo squeezed my hands and smiled at me.

"Perfect song," she said lightheartedly.

I got back to our conversation. "So, you're holding the bat and you see his suitcases. What happens next?"

"He yanked the bat from my hand. I lurched backward, tripped and fell down on his ugly brown and yellow linoleum floor. Larry threw the bat, grabbed his luggage, and turned to leave. I rolled onto my knees, retrieved the bat and swung hard with a direct hit to the back of both of his legs. He fell into the hallway and down the steps screaming and cursing."

"Lo, if he went to the ER, that's good news. The police would have taken his statement. You need to give them yours. It's not too late. But we have to do this now. We can fix this."

"I will take care of this myself, Dan. You have your ways, the police-department-handbook-training-manual ways. I found out after I phoned the hospital that he wasn't ever there. He never talked with the police. I will track him down. I will get Busha's ring no matter how long it takes."

Lo stood, kissed my forehead, seized my keys and ran to the door. I didn't try to stop her. I figured she would want to go solo. So I'll let her think that.

I watched as my truck swerved through the rain, ordered a refill, and recalled why she was named Loreli and why Lo forbid anyone to call her that. I thought it was because of the Marilyn Monroe character, Lorelei Lee, in Gentlemen Prefer Blondes: figured her mom was a movie buff. Found out she wasn't. Loreli told me, with an obvious distaste and a look associated with a speaker stretching the word *yuck*, that she was named after a legendary siren, often with a mermaid's tail, who lives on the rocks of the Rhine River and lures fishermen to their deaths with her song. I remembered my response— "Like the opposite of a lighthouse I guess?"

The waitress must have seen Lo's abrupt departure. She handed me the check and said, "You okay, hon?" I smiled at her. Then I dodged large puddles outside and thumbed a ride to Busha's. I wasn't surprised to see my truck parked outside.

CHAPTER 7

The Ring

———

LO WAS GONE, BUT BUSHA WAS RELIEVED TO SEE ME AND
eager to talk. Moving stiffly to the kitchen table, she began. "Lo is sometimes
like her mother, and this is bad. But most times she is normal, not like her
mother. Now, I worry. She is too upset. Might make mistakes. She tells me
nothing except, "I'll be fine." Out the door with a quick kiss. Lo helps keep
my feet on the floor. I think you would say she 'keeps me grounded'? Right?
Why is she not grounded?"

"Yes, right. Lo keeps you grounded, Busha," I added. Time was critical
so I asked her to continue.

"I give money to people, she gives information. She helps them. She
likes this investigating very much. Stubborn she is to find answers. They pay
her. I don't know how much because Lo buys very little for herself. It is for
me, Kazia, and a few others she shops."

"Busha," I interrupted. "Are you telling me that Lo is a private investi-
gator? I've been here for months and no one, not you, not Lo, no one ever
told me this. I had no idea. This time, Busha, she's dealing with Larry and
it's personal. Too many emotions involved make it harder to be rational, for
both of them. Lo's going after him because of your onyx ring. She told me its
history and she is determined to find him and return the ring to you. I need
you to tell me about him, where he might go, who his friends are. Lo needs
help whether she wants to admit it or not."

"Good, you find Lo, help her, bring her home but forget the ring. Too much trouble. I think danger and two people I love might get hurt. You both matter more. Ring is worthless."

Busha moved to her rocking chair and asked for herbal tea. The kettle shrieked, I poured the steaming water into a mug, swirled the tea bag then added honey. Busha was slumped with a multicolored shawl about her shoulders. I gave her the mug and pulled a chair close to her. I waited as she sipped and her body relaxed.

"I understand how you must feel, Busha. But the ring is valuable. Black onyx can be pricey, especially carved from one piece. And it's part of your culture's history. I want the ring back here, home with you, a part of your community. I want it as much as Lo does."

She nodded and I hoped this meant she accepted my argument. She started to speak, stopped, and sipped more tea.

"Busha, my policeman's instinct tells me there is more, something you're not telling me. Larry did steal the ring, didn't he?"

"I am ashamed," she answered, "and you will be upset with me. Sometimes I am not so smart. I act too fast. Regret later my stupidity. Worse, I convince myself I can help. I confuse myself between magic and real. Superstitious like ancient ways or truthful and honest. I get caught between them."

"We don't have much time, Busha. Tell me what you did."

"I gave to wretched Larry. It is what I do. I lend ring to him like I have always done with others. He was bruised, bleeding, and crying. Says he loves me and Lo. Will be good to us, always. But needs ring to help him be a 'better person' he says. I believed him."

So he left here with the ring, went home to pack, enter Lo, and bruised and bleeding sounds about right. I pictured the scene for a second time as I kissed Busha and told her not to worry.

I packed my gear; hesitated about whether to take my pistol. Maybe not. I might be tempted to use it. I got cash from my account, planned my route through the rural parts of a two state area, and left with every intention of getting this done quickly.

It would be months before I would see Lo walk into Larry's bar disguised as Sal.

CHAPTER 8

My Story

I HAVE A BAD HABIT: MY MIND WANDERS WHEN DRIVING becomes monotonous. When the roads are easy and with little traffic, boredom is replaced with musing, absorbed in thought, recalling memories and people from another time and place, like my family.

When I was three years old, I built a lego tower complex. My mother proclaimed me a genius; her gifted son who would make her proud one day. She called me her Danny Boy.

Ten years later, I shot my first songbird while it flew from a tree.

In between the years of genius and murderer, I had lost my mother, lived with a crazy bitch of an aunt along with her foul-mouthed brothers and worked in the hot fields of Alabama picking cotton instead of being in school. I ran away twice, was tracked down by a family with shotguns, caught naked while bathing in the Chattahoochee River, beaten and cursed and taken back to a home of degenerates. Next time, I promised myself, I would discard them like the trash they were. A year later, I hot wired their old blue Chevy and left while they succumbed to their alcoholic dreams.

I wished them undone like tokens placed upon a rock, my foot smashing and crushing them. They taught me how not to be. I learned from the worst examples of humanity to become a better person, one who will forgive most transgressions by either walking away or, if I care enough, work my ass off to correct…maybe to forgive and forget.

I love Lo and Busha. They brought out a nurturing I did not know I possessed. I am needed here in this small space of a community that cares about me. They smile, wave, and pause to chat with me. They rest their hand on my shoulder imparting a warmth through my old denim shirt, making me feel special. I will do whatever is necessary to maintain the stability of this place I call home. This family depends on me. They respect me. I will never abandon them.

CHAPTER 9

Case Closed

_____

AFTER SEVERAL MONTHS OF SEARCHING, OF FOLLOWING leads, of being disappointed over and over again, of thinking I was never going to find Larry or Lo, I saw his yellow Mustang in a parking lot with the sign Larry's Bar on the roof of dark planked wooden structure. Random good luck! There were other cars and a few trucks on the crushed stone lot, but Larry was careful to park his 'baby' at a distance, a place all its own. It was late afternoon and I was hauling wood for a local distributor in a company truck. I had quit the force and was working my way across the state, taking odd jobs to pay for my search for friend and foe.

I smiled, turned the volume up on my radio, revved the engine of my rig, and yelled, "Let's kiss that baby bye-bye!" I whooped as I accelerated past the bar's door and rammed the little car onto the grass and into some large tree trunks.

·Checking my review mirror, I hoped to see Larry propel through the door.

He did. The screaming and cursing faded as I disappeared.

Two miles down the road, I too was cursing: what the hell was the matter with me?

Celebrating in my motel room with a Natty Boh, I decided to have no regrets. I did it, he deserved it, and I would find Lo. I suspected that Larry probably had no idea I was driving the truck. I could be wrong. I needed to be careful.

I showed up at the bar on different days. I tried afternoons and late evenings for two weeks. I wore different plaid shirts over a small pillow held in place with my belt, walked with a limp and kept a low profile. You know this next part: Lo entered the bar and entertained the large crowd gathered for half-priced burgers. I knew it was her even with the sultry look and phony accent. She definitely mastered the regional sound. She was better at concealing her identity. Sal, aka Lo, was proving to be a good partner. We had found our enemy.

Our plan was simple: wait in the parking lot for the bar to empty. We would finish this tonight. In the early morning hours, we entered. Larry wasn't surprised to see us. Was he playing a game too? I may have underestimated him. Then he spoke. "Hey. Where's your costume Lo? Loreli? Sal?"

He stepped from behind the bar with a baseball bat clutched in his right fist. Seems to be the weapon of choice around here and I was grateful it did not involve bullets.

"I knew you were in town, Dan. Two weeks ago, my Mustang, new patron in plaid shirts and big-sized pants! I so wanted to hurt you but I had to be patient figuring Lo would show up too. And here we are, on my territory and with my terms. Hear that noise, Dan? My guys are messing with your precious, cheap Chevy S 10 pickup."

"That's fair," I hardly could believe my own words.

"Larry, we have a few questions. We've worked hard to find you. Can I buy a bottle of your best whiskey? Can we sit down and talk?" I asked.

"I don't think we can because this is going to be quick."

To prove otherwise, Lo and I sat down. Larry grunted and did likewise.

Larry said, "I want to explain about my mother. I know how you are, Lo, alway wanting answers, worrying about your 'community.' My mother is safe. She is in a clean, assisted living center, loves the place but has no idea who I am. She has a boyfriend, Sid. They write notes to each other, completely illegible except for one word: love. They hold hands and smile. I should have handled it better, let you and others know about her. That day, I was pissed at everybody, people I don't even know, the world, myself. Too many busybodies, young and old. I know you think they care. I disagree."

"Glad you told me about your mother. If only they knew, the people in the neighborhood loved and cared for her. You hurt them and they deserved better. Yes, you should have handled it better, like an adult. Good you're in a sharing mood because I have a question; did you spike my drink the night of our phony marriage? It hurts to even say the word *marriage*. I need to gargle, clean out my mouth."

She gulped her beer then said, "You did, didn't you?"

"Not one of my better moments. I regret it. I am sorry. But, Lo, you were crazy wild. It was to calm you, make you manageable. It didn't. And I was flying high myself, nervous about getting us married. You know how I feel about you, Lo. When you said yes to meeting me, I was going to talk, have a civil conversation like we'd done before. I had to know how serious things were getting between you and him," Larry said as he used his chin to point in my direction.

Lo took her turn, leaned into the table bringing her face close to Larry's. "Stop with all the 'I regret and I'm sorry.' It's what you do. You'll never change. You upset the people around you, the people who care about your mother, your irrational behavior because you need to know about me and Dan! I'm telling you: you do not need to know about us! You need to grow up! It's none of your damn business. Understanding human behavior is beyond you, Larry. No empathy, ever, only self-absorbed in your tiny place in the universe. This bar, with your name in neon, is probably one of the best ideas you ever had."

Lo leaned back into her chair and in a calmer tone continued. "You're a bartender. You hear your customers' worries, their fears and concerns. Do you care as you fill their shot glasses to the rims? You soothe them with spirits and wipe down the bar. Have you learned nothing? It's been months since you left. Surely you've come to recognize how people suffer and are tormented and burdened in their lives."

"Tsk, tsk, Lo. You've been analyzing me. Another field of expertise?"

Larry placed his arms across his chest, appeared bored, then spoke. "We're not married. No paperwork, only missing cash. Yes, I am scum. I put something in your drink and drove to a motel. Your brain snapped, like pressing on an accelerator. You threw lamps, you fell, I leaned to pick you up, landed on top of you. With the strength of an ox you heaved me up and over and landed a hard punch to my face. Later that night, you would punch me again! Lucky me. You passed out on the bed in the motel. I cried in pain then limped to the manager's office. Know where I ended up, don't you?"

"Not the emergency room," I said.

"Who asked you? This is between me and Lo. Pretend you're not here. Better yet, go. Wait outside."

I responded by going behind the bar and pouring myself a double of Jim Beam. I lingered there, studying the labels, read a scribbled note, and looked under the counter. I killed some time. I wondered how Busha might corrupt that expression...*time is murdering me?* I listened to their conversation, poured another double and went to the old coffee pot at the end of the bar.

"I never went to the ER. You had passed out so I carried you to my car, put you in the back, and went to see Busha. Dan, pour us shots and let me tell you what I learned about the ring," Larry said.

"Sounds like you don't have it, Larry," I added as I brought the bottle and glasses to the table.

Larry grinned. When he spoke each word was emphasized. The musical term is *staccato*. A gangster term is gunfire, as in bullets finding their intended target. His words, ammunition, hit Lo. "Busha... gave... me... the... ring."

I had neglected to tell Lo about this last night. I had to wait to see what happened, didn't want to upset her. Maybe a mistake...

"Never," Lo shouted. "Never would happen in a million years."

"But your kind-hearted Busha did. You were in my car, unconscious. I went to her, told her I needed help. I didn't mention it was about you, Lo. People go to Busha, tell her things. Confessions with Father Rolanski are for sins he will understand. He is old and, I've been told, falls asleep on his side of the confessional. Your people save really important, complicated issues for Busha who handles things. Like you, Lo."

"Larry, you are not telling me Busha listened and took pity on you. How is that possible?" Lo asked.

"I was a mess. You're stronger than you look and the punch you gave me, well, hurt like hell. I cried. Don't look so shocked. I'm human. I was patient, let her talk on and on about you. I was getting restless and also worried you might come in and ruin everything. She held the ring; I was getting nervous that she would change her mind. She gave me instructions about how to use it properly. I almost laughed. Yes, Lo, I took advantage of her good nature. I was certain my having the ring would bring you to me. Took you longer than I thought it would, Miss-not-so-smart private detective!"

I wanted to hit him. So did Lo: she was rising from her chair. Larry raised both hands and said, "Calm down you two. Can't a guy have some fun at your expense? It's the kinda person I am, right Lo? Relax, I'm almost finished. I thanked Busha and left. You were still unconscious in the back seat, so I drove back to my apartment, packed, and then you came through the door and again overreacted."

"I overreacted? Can't help yourself, can you, Larry? You go crazy and it's my fault! I saw Busha's ring on your finger and, absolutely, I reacted! I want her ring!"

"Your grandmother would forgive me. We both know it. Why can't you be like her?"

Lo, eyes searching his face, then mine, tried to deal with Larry's remarks.

"You don't know her as well as you think. She lent you the ring like she does with everybody else. She expects it back. Forgiving? You see things through your own defensive prism. Do you think she would forgive you if I told her about the pretend marriage, the one you wanted so badly, you drugged me. You're a criminal, Larry. A deviant. Get me the ring. Now!"

"Larry, why didn't you explain all this when Lo came to your apartment?" I asked.

"You're kidding right, Dan? She punched me, for the second time that night, grabbed a bat, and charged in. What would you do, *officer*?"

Not an officer any more, I wanted to say.

"Let's all have another drink. There's more to tell you," Larry suggested.

I went and poured three cups of coffee. I was worried what else Larry had to say, thought we should be prepared, but with less booze. Police instinct. I took my time, rooted around the shelves under the bar, and looked into boxes. Lo got up, walked behind Larry, grabbed his arm, turned it quickly and held it hard against his back while pushing his head into the table. I definitely wanted her on my team.

"Get me the ring now, before I really hurt you," she yelled.

I got there just in time to disable Larry's defensive move when he shouted "I don't have the damn ring!"

Everything stopped, a complete, silent stillness. Quiet. Disbelief. Lo and I sat down and waited.

Larry jerked free, glared at Lo. "You are such a bitch. But I still love you."

Her face said, *Shut up and start talking.*

He read the expression and said, "I bought this bar from a guy who played at being a collector: e-bay, garage, or estate sales, anywhere he could find cool stuff. 'Unique' he told me when he saw the ring. I told him it was onyx. He insisted it was not. He knew onyx he told me, and this was not it. He then had it assayed and discovered it was anthracite. Yeah, coal, but with a submetallic luster and covered with a transparent material used on gemstones. He was intrigued, so I traded it for a discount on the purchase price for my bar. End of story. That's all I know."

Lo looked defeated.

I tapped her knee, she turned and looked my way. I smiled and winked. She peered intently into my eyes, moved even closer, and the creases in her forehead told me that she was trying hard to figure me out. When she smiled, I didn't have to say another word.

Without speaking we rose, started to leave when Larry smiled and said, "Come here tomorrow for breakfast. I owe you that much before you head home."

As we walked toward the door, I held Lo's hand tightly, very tightly, so she could feel the ring press into her flesh. I had found it under the bar. Larry, the liar, had lost this battle. We swung our hands back and forth playing with the thought of an ending and a new beginning. At the door, she turned to me and putting her hands around my neck, drew me even closer. We kissed.

"Get outta here, you two. See you tomorrow?"

"Probably not," we answer simultaneously.

My old truck, now totally destroyed on the parking lot, tarnished our victory. Briefly. I hot-wired Larry's new Mustang, revved the engine and as crushed stone flew beneath its wheels the bar door slammed opened. His guttural scream, the raising of fists, and stomping of feet resulted. Lo rested her hand on my thigh and said, "Something must have upset him."

Afternoon Delight

SAM LOVED MOLLY. TWO KIDS, JANE AND TOM, AND FIFTEEN years of marriage made him love her even more. He wanted to love her in the early morning hours any day between Monday through Friday, or during a more reasonable time on Saturday or Sunday. He would gently rub her back and shoulders, hoping he could keep her with him … that maybe she might resist her usual urge to jump out of bed to begin her day. She was a school teacher and believed in keeping to a schedule.

With his practiced touch, Molly imagined Sam playing an instrument, knowing her body and fine tuning it. "Hmm," she purred, until his hand drifted to more intimate regions.

"Not now, later," she offered. They both knew what Molly desired: black coffee, newspaper, more coffee, shower and chores.

On this particular Saturday, after the morning ritual of being refused yet again, Sam replied, "That's what you always say. But when is later?"

"Three o'clock," Molly yelled from the bathroom.

Sam cheerfully volunteered to do the grocery shopping, assigned Jane and Tom their chores and asked Molly to make him a "to-do" list for when he returned. She smiled, reached for her garden hat and gloves, then spent time tending her perennial flower beds. Whenever Sam saw one of the kids approaching her, he called, "Don't bother your mother. Can't you see she's busy? Tell *me* what you want."

Molly overheard and concluded the anticipation of sex was a powerful motivator.

She smiled, hummed and cut a bouquet of daisies for Jane's bedroom.

Sam thought, *Is it 3 o'clock yet?*

Molly fixed egg salad for lunch at 1:30 and the children shared their plans after chores were completed—fishing for Tom with his friend at the pond near the high school while Jane and her friends would talk about a starting a club. This was Jane's suggestion because, as she had explained to them, "I want to be president of something."

Sam and Molly exchanged a knowing glance, stifled their enthusiasm, and nodded slowly, trying to be interested in the conversation. Sam leaned into Molly, moved a stray curl from her face and tucked it behind her ear, allowing his fingers to softly trace the area down her neck.

"Mom? Dad? Are you listening?" asked Jane.

They nodded, and the children began talking over each other, eager to explain the details, excited to have both parents listening and smiling.

Under the table, Molly placed her hand on Sam's thigh. He squared his shoulders and inhaled audibly.

"What Dad?" Tom asked. "Did you want to go with us?"

"Not today, son, I've made plans. Maybe another day and…"

"Me too," Molly interrupted, causing all heads to turn in her direction.

She blushed, stammered, and said, "Plans, I have plans … which do not include cooking or cleaning. I am going to bed," the redness deepened, "to take a nap!"

The kids were gone, yet they moved quietly up the steps, expecting an interruption. Something so different for both of them was about to take place: being in bed, together, in the middle of the day! They practiced caution; took no chances.

Sam smiled as he lowered the shade then laid down just as Molly had entered the bedroom.

"NO!" yelled Molly as she grabbed Sam's shirt, buttoning it as she bolted down the steps.

"WHAT? WHAT IS IT?" He yelled.

"It's the doors … I have to lock them. What if they came in while … well, you know," she yelled as her foot reached the landing. There were five entry ways and Sam, listening at the top of the stairs, heard four clicks and a "there now" pronounced after each one.

She was on the first step when he said, "Molly, did you check the basement door?"

"Damn!" And, once again, fast footsteps.

She approached the solid steel door and heard her son's voice on the other side. "Give me a sec, I'll check in the basement. I think we have one," he was saying to his friend.

Molly turned and crouched under the stairway.

"Never mind. I found one, Tom," his friend called. "Let's go!"

His retreat was followed by her retreat after she locked the door.

Catching her breath, Molly stood in the bedroom's doorway, looked at Sam and said, "What? You have something smart to say, Mister?"

"Get in this bed now," he demanded then added as she lay back and laughed. "You locked the kids out of the house? Is that legal? Smart, yes, but legal?"

On their sides, they kissed, then giggled at the newness of their adventure.

"I am proud of us," Sam whispered.

Their hands wandered along the other's body, down the slope to the waist and slowly up the curve of the hip. They repeated the motion. Sam moved his hand to the back of Molly's neck and softly stroked the long auburn curls covering her shoulder. Breathing became shallow. He was making her happy, he could tell. Opening his eyes, he saw Molly had fallen asleep.

She awakened at 3:50 to Sam's snoring.

"What crazy and wild lovers we are," she whispered.

His eyes opened drowsily and locked on hers. "It's time to be primitive!" he growled through a teasing smile.

"Primitive, my dearest? Please proceed."

And he did.

Sam unlocked the front door and grinned because it went so perfectly. "If only we knew—if only we had tried this before…"

Molly came from behind and wrapped her arms around his waist. "Well, now we know. It reminds me of a romantic comedy with my running up and down the steps and both of us falling asleep. Our movie, starring you and me, and we'll call it Afternoon Delight."

"Isn't that the name of a perfume or a new ice cream?" he asked.

"No, it is not," she laughed. "But it can be our private code for next time, don't you think?"

"You betcha," he answered while opening the front door for Jane who was running up the driveway to the front steps.

Cut the Cake

I WAS SEVEN AND LOOKING FORWARD TO EGG HUNTS AND chocolate bunnies when Mom announced we were going to her sister Edna's for dinner. Church was over, we were in our green station wagon and not going home for our Easter dinner! This had never happened before.

My older brother, Michael, moaned and Dad paused, the key not making it to the ignition. Last Easter, they visited us for dinner and my brother and I had met our Aunt's family for the first time.

Mom did not turn, and looking straight ahead, she said, "Aunt Edna called two days ago to invite us. I apologize for not letting you know sooner. This is important to me. My sister is returning the favor because we invited them last year. I hope the spirit of Easter and the Christian fellowship we just experienced will help you to understand. Michael, you can change your clothes and play ball when we get home. Marie, the chocolate bunny is a treat I know you have been anticipating for days. It will be sweeter if tasting is delayed. Please, can you all do this for me?"

She had not addressed my father but continued sitting, waiting for the motor to start I imagined. It did not. I looked at Michael and he gave me his what-happens-next face.

Dad gazed in Mom's direction. Her head bent slightly to him and I could see a hint of a smile. Then with a shrug of his shoulders, the engine purred and gears shifted.

Looking back at us, Mom spoke.

"Remember, Michael and Marie, your aunt and uncle are fussy people, and for them to invite us is quite a privilege, unusual even. Mind your P's and Q's, don't touch anything, use your best manners, say please and thank you and above all, do not speak to them unless they speak to you first. That last one is a 'just in case.' You both have good manners. I'm being cautious I suppose. In other words, have a good time but don't make them sorry they invited us. Let's all have a good time," she concluded, glancing in my father's direction.

"P's and Q's, you two," Dad repeated.

And so the hour drive began.

We were welcomed into their house with a quick greeting, hugs but no kisses, and a hasty removal of our jackets.

"Come in, come in, come in," blustered Aunt Edna excitedly.

The hallway of the small house was crowded as we removed jackets and piled them into Uncle Theo's waiting arms. The door shut, the sunshine disappeared and we inched forward into the living room, still passing coats and hats in the narrow front hall.

My eyes struggled to adjust to the dim interior. The small room was darkened by heavy, closed drapes. I barely missed bumping into a small table burdened with knickknacks, turned to avoid it, and became entangled with Michael. He was generally the clumsy one, so Mom glared at him, but placed a firm hand on both of our shoulders.

"I can't see," whined my brother.

"My God, Theo, is it always this dark in here?" Dad stated firmly.

With disagreeable grunts, Uncle Theo yanked open the drapes.

We gaped at the scene before us. The room was crowded and cramped with a collection of chairs and tables of various sizes holding lamps and tiny glass figurines of dogs, cats, children, birds in flight or nesting. The lamps had fringe or baubles hanging from their shades which rained down upon the menagerie resting below. I wandered closer with an outstretched hand hoping to inspect the beautiful child with golden curls as she stroked a spotted cat sleeping in her lap. The blue ribbon of her bonnet lay untied upon her white laced dress and I had never seen anything so desirable.

Quietly, Mom called my name. I turned and she patted the plastic covered seat next to her on the sofa. As she did so, Michael plopped into its crinkly sound. He rubbed his hand back and forth across the plastic, pressing his sweaty palm harder as a strange noise trumpeted its way through the room.

"Hey, look Mom, this is so cool. How come we don't have stuff like this on our furniture?"

Our cousins, Helen and Betty, giggled from the hallway, straightened their backs, and came to greet my parents with a hasty hug. With cranky faces, they nodded our way before they sat down upon floral fabric chairs sending dust particles through the beam of sunshine.

Aunt Edna squirmed uncomfortably.

Uncle Theo sneezed, reached for his handkerchief and sneezed several times in succession.

We sat there, pretending to rearrange ourselves while we waited for conversation to begin.

Dad straightened, cleared his throat, and began to speak, but Aunt Edna clapped her hands, smiled broadly, and said, "I have something special to show you all. You're going to like this. But Michael, please keep your hands by your sides; no touching my handiwork. Follow me, follow me everyone, please follow."

Which wasn't very far, because she stood, took one step into the dining room, and came round to face us.

I like surprises but was uncertain about handiwork. She was excited and I took this as a very good sign and leaped to be in front. Aunt Edna's heavy chest was inches away from my nose. Dangling there was a delicate chain that held a small cross covered with little pieces of sparkling glass. My mother had the same one, so I knew about the viewing spot where the two parts of the cross intersect. Mom would let me peer through hers and see the words of The Our Father.

I looked behind me to see Michael, Mom, Dad, my cousins, and Uncle Theo in a line.

Aunt Edna is playing a game and acting like a school teacher taking us outside for recess and a treat. This is going to be fun.

When she stepped aside and switched on the chandelier, I was breathless and rooted to the green carpet. Michael was surprised, too, because I heard him say, "Oh dear God, Holy Mother Mary" … when Mom's hand clamped over his mouth.

Blanketing the table like a Christmas village in spring, were lamb and rabbit cakes of different shapes and sizes, all with a deliciously smooth white frosting. Near the edge of the table was a resting lamb covered in coconut and smiling at me with her eyes of pink gumdrops. I expected her candied nose to twitch in greeting. She lay upon a platter of green tinted coconut with jelly beans sprinkled about. Nearby, a white rabbit with a rich lustrous coat stood on its hind legs with delicate paws bent. Her head was turned, as if looking over her shoulder, checking to see admiring onlookers like me. Cakes! Wonderful cakes! As I reached my fingers toward the rabbit, Aunt Edna's hand came down upon mine with a squeeze. She looked over my head to my mother, sighed loudly, then snapped, "Marie, be a good girl now and don't touch anything."

Shouldn't she have looked at me instead of Mom? I asked myself.

Her interruption was soon forgotten as I noticed more of her marvelous creatures—two rabbits that sat facing each other, maybe getting ready to rabbit kiss. I wanted to pet them. And I wanted to taste them, too. We paraded around the table and I could tell my family was impressed. Questions were asked and compliments given. Their voices were a blur. I studied the stunning display. My heart warmed toward Aunt Edna for inviting us. I licked my lips in anticipation. I studied all of the chocolate eggs that lay between the luscious cakes.

In the very center of the table and sitting on an upside down bowl was a very big egg whose top almost touched the chandelier. I memorized all of its contents that first Easter. It sparkled as it reflected the light from above. Two large oval openings were on sides opposite of each other so that I could see Helen across the table, waving at me through the egg.

"Astonishing," I whispered to no one as I recalled my favorite vocabulary word from Mrs. Dodson's class.

Inside the egg were tiny painted figures of ducklings and rabbits, grass and flowering trees, a bridge going over a stream and on it, an Easter Rabbit holding a small, white wicker basket. Every piece glistened as if coated by magic. I felt poetic: such wonderfulness in this ordinary room, but made extraordinary by the decorations before me. I studied and searched, afraid of missing something. When I saw a new piece, I whispered it. And when I finished the list, I started all over again. I circled the table. I would have lingered longer, wanted to, but my father nudged me into the kitchen and toward the food.

"You may look again later, Marie," he leaned and whispered in my ear. "Aunt Edna says dinner is ready. Remember, P's and Q's."

Michael was heaping mashed potatoes onto his plate when Mom said, "Here, Michael, let me do that." And she removed half of what he had taken and then prepared a dish for me.

"Where's the lamb, Aunt Edith?" asked Michael.

"Here, Michael, is a nice slice of ham," Dad said as he forked a piece on Michael's plate.

"No, Dad, I said lamb, not..." but Michael was cut off by Dad guiding him to the vegetables.

There wasn't any lamb. To Michael and me, that was like Thanksgiving without the turkey and dressing. We thought everybody ate lamb for Easter, but I guess that's not true.

Uncle Theo led us into the den, a room with dark paneling and one overhead light. There were folding chairs arranged in a circle along with trays.

"Don't spill your milk," he said to Michael and me.

We sat tightly fitted into the room with tray touching tray and everyone talking about Aunt Edna's display. I told her I thought handiwork was lots of fun and I would like to try it myself. She beamed and smiled as we ate and continued to remark about the display. I emptied my plate, even the string beans and beets. I ate without tasting. I was dreaming about dessert. I would choose the lamb cake. I wanted to know the taste of beauty.

I stood to help clear the dishes like I do at home. But as I reached for the forks, Uncle Theo's eyes turned on me, I sat back down, and he mumbled, "You're too young; you might drop something."

The adults removed the dishes slowly, as the tightness of the doorway and the narrowness of the hall between the den and the kitchen did not allow for a quick undertaking.

When they returned, they had coffee and a tray of cookies. I would wait for the cakes. I can always eat cookies. Uncle Theo and Dad were sharing workplace complaints while Mom and Aunt Edna relived childhood memories.

I was figuring how best to leave the room and wander back to the dining room when I heard Aunt Edna's tone change.

Aunt Edna and Mom returned my look with adult eyes, suggesting I should not be listening. I turned in my chair, saw a book nearby, picked it up and placed it in my lap. I flipped its pages. I moved my lips a bit, acted the part of being immersed, and listened.

Aunt Edna spoke. "I'm remembering Mother's 65th birthday. I gave her yet another bathrobe even though I gave her one the year before and perhaps the year before that. I could think of nothing else. You knew she needed a sweater. I hadn't noticed. Her face flushed as she excitedly put it on, its soft pink cashmere matching her blushing cheeks. You and I are so different and I always felt I should try to be like you, then frustrated myself trying."

"Edna, let's not go through this again, please. Not here, not now. You and I have made amends. We understand each other and appreciate our likes and differences. We are the only family that is left and I love you, Edna."

Both women fingered their crosses. Aunt Edna, chewing her bottom lip, cleared her throat then spoke softly.

"Ethel, you remind me of Mother. She used to put her hand on my shoulder, look into my eyes, and say, 'Put things right between us'. She humbled me with kind words, explaining a better way to think about matters which irritated me. I brood, Ethel. I take small matters and give them too much importance. Why do I make myself so miserable? I love this cross you gave me after Mother's death. 'Her favorite prayer' you told me. I pretended to know, but never realized she even had a favorite prayer. This is not the time or place, you are right, Ethel. I promise there will never again be the time or place for such trivial matters."

They leaned their heads until they touched and when Aunt Edna's arm slipped around my mother's shoulders, I saw tears in their eyes.

Sitting, waiting, growing restless, I pumped my knee up and down. Michael was shifting back and forth. Betty, looking even crankier, nudged him with her elbow and whispered, "Sit still, moron."

Michael excused himself to go to the bathroom. Good idea I thought, and when he returned, I did the same thing by way of the dining room, of course. As I daydreamed a story in which all of the cakes were characters, Uncle Theo tapped my shoulder so I returned to join the others.

Time passed slowly. Watching P's and Q's was not easy. At our house, we would have been outside playing with cousins while waiting to be called in for dessert. Here, we were expected to sit and be quiet. Or as Uncle Theo had said to us earlier, "No running around outside in our yard. Don't want the grass trampled or the plants broken."

Michael was again fidgeting beside me and Uncle Theo was looking nervously at Aunt Edna. He rose from his chair and started to remove our trays.

Mom and Dad both stood, called our names, and moved toward the front closet.

"Wait, Mom. She didn't cut the cakes." I said. "Dad? She didn't cut the cakes," I repeated louder, looking from one to the other.

"What's the problem, Ethel?" Aunt Edna demanded.

"You haven't cut the cake! We haven't had our cake!" I said louder. "I want the lamb cake! I was a good girl and I want the cake, please. May I have my cake, Aunt Edna?"

"Shameful behavior!" snapped Uncle Theo. " 'My cake,' she says. After all that work? You want us to cut them? I think not! You don't cut cakes like that, you silly girl!"

"She's not a silly girl, Theo. She's a sensitive one," Dad said softly.

"My mother will cut them for you, Aunt Edna, if you can't. Let my mother cut the cake, the lamb cake. You'll cut the cake for them won't you, Mom?"

She leaned down and with her ironed white handkerchief wiped my nose and tears.

"She didn't cut the cake, Mom. All I want is a small piece of lamb cake. Please, Mom, can't I have a small piece of cake?"

My father whisked me into his arms and out the door. Good-byes were given quickly because in minutes the car was heading home. I was still crying. My mother sat with me in the backseat and stroked my hair.

"Marie, you're a good girl and Aunt Edna and Uncle Theo know that. Aunt Edna disappointed you, I know. We all would have liked to try one of those cakes. I have never made a cake like that, and I am sure Uncle Theo was right when he said they were a lot of work. Be a good girl, Marie, and try to understand and forgive them for not wanting to cut their cakes."

"But, Mom, even if they were hard work, wouldn't *they* want to eat them? What good are cakes if you don't eat them?" Michael asked.

"I wish I knew the answer to that, Michael," she said.

"Are they being selfish and not wanting to share with us?" I asked, still cuddled in my mother's arms.

"Oh, no. It's not that. Aunt Edna and Uncle Theo are generous people. As a matter of fact, they are dedicated to their church and volunteer often. Maybe they are donating them to the church for the evening meal served to the poor and needy. I'll bet that's the reason."

We were invited to Easter dinner for several years afterward and my mother always accepted. The sisters planned the menu on the phone two weeks before. They talked long and Mom laughed and jotted notes. When she hung up, she was smiling and humming.

The annual plan was for Mom to take lemon meringue pies and a leg of lamb, seasoned and tied, ready to place in the oven as soon as we arrived. Aunt Edna had ham and side dishes and always a platter of cupcakes from the bakery which she served with ice cream.

I gradually grew accustomed to admiring the cakes I would never taste. It was a touchy subject and now that Easter had become a celebration with both families, it was better left forgotten.

I was fourteen when we would celebrate Easter there for the last time. Aunt Edna passed away and future Easters would be spent at our home with Uncle Theo, Helen, and Betty. The girls insisted on bringing cupcakes and ice cream for dessert. "After all," Helen said as Betty nodded in agreement, "it is our tradition."

During one Easter dinner, while Helen and I were spooning ice cream and placing cupcakes on plates, I could not help myself. The words were spoken before I realized it.

"Helen," I whispered. "What happened to all of the cakes?"

"What cakes? Oh, sure. The lambs and rabbits. Marie, I have no idea!" she nervously replied.

"You don't know?" I asked surprised.

"Marie, please. I can't talk about it. Betty and I enjoyed looking at them."

"You mean you never tasted them either? You never ate any of the cake?"

And before she could answer, Uncle Theo came in to pour the coffee.

For the next six years, Uncle Theo, Helen, and Betty came to our house for the annual Easter dinner. Our numbers grew after I married and had two children. My cousins were loving aunts who liked to walk to the park with our children after dinner. The four of them came home laughing and tired from playing on swings and slides. Helen and Betty saw them only once a year, but they managed to make each visit special, bringing them gifts, playing board games, or going to the park.

When Uncle Theo passed away shortly before Easter, I was invited to visit Helen and Betty who were planning on selling their parents' house. They thought I might be interested in selecting an item of theirs as a keepsake. The timing was perfect since I had planned on helping my parents get their house ready to sell before they moved to a senior living facility.

I rang the doorbell with a bit of apprehension. It had been a long time since my last visit here. Betty answered with a bright smile and a crisp cotton dress.

We hugged. She invited me to walk through the downstairs rooms and if I did not mind, she would continue working upstairs with Helen to box her father's clothes.

The drapes were pulled back and sunlight filled the room where the same knickknacks remained, including the child with blond curls. I picked her up, smiled, and sat her back in the same spot defined by a dusty outline.

I was wondering why I had come. Nothing here appealed to me, except for the cakes. This house seemed distant, like a country not yet discovered. Easter dinners had gotten better, but the space was still somber like the people who had lived here and now were gone.

Then I saw them. The cake molds were stacked among other pots and pans, a coffee urn, and folded linens on the dining room table. I picked up the lamb mold, which looked much smaller than I remembered. The rabbit molds, one inside the other, were there as well. Altogether I counted ten molds. There were two of each kind of mold. Strange, I thought. Wouldn't she have used the same mold twice? What could possibly be the reason for the double molds?

"Remember those?" Helen asked, startling me. "I just brought them up from the basement an hour ago. What a fuss you caused. My parents complained about your behavior for weeks. Do you want any of the cake molds? The rabbit one? All of them?"

Ignoring her questions, I asked, "Helen, did you ever eat the cakes? Any of them?"

"No."

"Why? What happened to all of the marvelous cakes she made?"

"Let's sit down and have some tea. Clear a spot and I'll call Betty. We need a break."

I picked up the lamb mold and imagined how it looked so many years ago. A fleck of pink color caught my eye and I picked it loose from the outside of the mold. A thought was forming as my cousins came to the table and we sat down.

Helen began.

"My mother never enjoyed house work, Marie. She worked as a book-keeper when we were in high school. She liked her job and said numbers made sense to her. If the books were off by even one penny, which did not happen often, she worked happily until the error was found."

"Mom often mentioned your mother whenever she felt obligated to clean house. 'Ethel loves this kind of thing,' she would mumble under her breath. 'Well, I'm not Ethel and never will be.' She didn't like being in the kitchen, didn't enjoy baking or cooking. She had a small collection of recipes for dinners. A basic meatloaf, a pot roast recipe, and baked chicken. But she was not in the same league as your mother."

"We talked about your Mom's first Easter dinner as we drove home. Our Dad liked the roasted leg of lamb with garlic. He said he had never had lamb, thought he wouldn't like it, and 'served with mint jelly! What a surprise!' He enjoyed your Mom's vegetables too, which was unusual for him. 'What did she do, Edna, to make them so good?' I remember him asking. Mom mum-bled something about herbs, then tried to change the subject. It didn't work because then Betty recalled your Mom's dining room table with fresh flowers and matching dishes. I chimed in something about the sideboard filled with cakes and pies that she baked. My Mom was quiet as we continued to savor the experience."

"Our dishes matched?" I responded with pride as I recalled how it pleased Mom to set the table for special dinners.

Betty smiled and said, "As we arrived at our neighborhood, Mom announced she would invite your family for next Easter dinner. Helen and I looked at each other, each of his filled with doubt. We never again mentioned our visit, hoping Mom would forget, realizing how difficult this might be for her to do. A month before Easter she started a list, searched for ideas from magazines and ordered several cake molds in different poses and sizes. When the tin molds arrived, Helen and I were amazed and relieved Mom had decided to be so creative. I was sure your family would be impressed and I was proud of my mother for her originality."

I said, "I was awestruck by her cakes and recall Mom's many compliments and Dad's nudging Uncle Theo with a thumb's up and a handshake. They were magnificent, and I could not wait to taste them. So why didn't I? Why didn't she cut the cake?" I was hearing the echo of my younger self say.

"Because, Marie, there was no cake!"

I looked from one to the other.

Helen nodded as Betty said, "On Easter morning of your first visit, we came downstairs and saw the table filled with decorated animal cakes displayed amidst all of the colored grasses along with our baskets wrapped in cellophane. They told us the cakes were decorations, only to be looked at. We decided to spy when it was her turn to host the next Easter dinner."

Betty's voice was edged with laughter as she said with excitement, "It was fun, trying to solve the mystery. We played girl detectives just like the books we read. One night, while we were in our beds, we knew to be alert because they whispered to each other that day, or stopped a conversation when we came nearby. We heard them giggling! Rare, never heard them do that! We, too, were giggling and smiling with anticipation. I was nervous, anxious about what I might learn. But not Helen. She's the bold one, but then she's older than me!"

Helen laughed, elbowed her sister, and boasted, "Sure, I am a natural born leader, sweet Betty. But I would be nothing without you!"

"Enough sister-bonding, cousins. What happened? What did you learn?"

Betty began. "We heard clattering noises coming from the kitchen. We tiptoed so we could see them from the stairway and watched as they frosted *the metal molds!* You're mouth just dropped, Marie! So did ours! We saw some had already been frosted and others, yet to be frosted, on the counter. They were taped closed. Our parents did not smile much, but they were now. They were having fun. We crept back to our beds and in whispery, sing-song voices, chorused your words, 'She didn't cut the cake' then added, because she *couldn't cut* the cake!"

"It's time to tell the rest of the story," Helen said. Betty looked puzzled. "You both should know this: Mom did try to make the cakes at least once, for the first dinner. I know because I saw the mess when I came quietly in the front door hoping not be noticed. I skinned my knee roller skating. Mom would get hysterical if we got the slightest cut or injury. I heard sniffling and mumbling in the kitchen. I eased my way to the door and peeked in at an array of ingredients and a mixer bowl. Flour dusted Mom's hair and clothes. Smoke was coming from the oven where the batter must have oozed through the two tin parts. She was pulling out the cake pans when one slipped and more batter burned on the bottom of the range and spilled onto the floor as she lost her balance, grabbed for the table, and pulled down a dozen eggs when she fell. 'I quit, I quit, I quit,' she screamed. Mom often said things in a series of three, didn't she? She did try and I thought it better, for her sake, to say nothing."

"I guess after that experience she bought more molds and went for her spectacular non-cake dessert display! And who can blame her?" Betty laughed.

My memory, altered forever now, left me with a sense of relief. I was awed by their majestic presentation. I saw, I felt, I reacted to their display just as I now experienced their laughter and fun in creating it. Now, as I heard their story I see them through a different prism, like the ones on the chandelier that created a drama of dancing colors on the cake scene below.

I recalled the large, oval-shaped, hollowed egg with openings on two sides underneath the chandelier.

"Please, one more thing?" I asked hoping my cousins had more time to talk.

"Sure, Marie, we're in no hurry. This is great, being with you, remembering our parents. You agree, Helen?"

"I don't want this to end," Helen admitted.

"I loved the large egg in the center of the table. Remember we waved to each other through its opened area, Helen? I wanted to own it and all of the pieces inside. It sparkled, glittered, and reminded me of magic. I think I can still name every item and where it was placed," I said.

"Me too," Helen sighed, "because I helped Mom shop for them. I was with her and she let me pick most of the pieces. She said I could help her arrange them. But then she forgot."

Helen stood, pulled mugs from a shelf and began filling them with coffee at the counter.

Betty put a finger to her lips indicating for me not to speak. But I did.

"Helen, what do you mean? She forgot?"

She returned with our coffees and smiled at her sister. "Betty, I'm ok. I understand that Mom and Dad were distant, sometimes lost in their own world, and rarely in ours. Insisting we sit like adults when dressed in our good clothes. That annoyed me! And Michael too!" She laughed.

We sipped our coffees in silence. My cousins seemed deep in thought and I did not want to interrupt.

"Marie," Helen said looking straight ahead, "she forgot to let me help her. I listened as she argued with herself about the placement of the tiny rabbits, chicks, and ducks. 'Here, no there, wrong, where?' with each one she held. I wanted her to notice I was with her. I remember whispering my wish for where the white rabbit in the checked vest should be and was delighted when she placed it in precisely that spot! I was afraid to remind her of our plan to do this together."

Moments passed in silence and I refilled our mugs, walked over to the molds, lifted one, and placed it in front of Helen. An idea had been forming while I listened to their story and I gave it voice.

"Betty, Helen, we can't change the past, but we can change the present: let's create a new memory and bake the cakes. Right now. Here. The three of us. Or make that four. Mom will want to be in on this. We certainly have enough molds and we can use every one of them to make delicious cakes beautifully frosted and decorated."

"Really? Are you sure? Do you have the time?" Betty asked.

"I will make the time! Michael is painting our parents' house before putting it on the market. He and Dad won't want to miss this! We'll figure it out together and bake, frost, and decorate Easter cakes. It'll be fun *and we can cut a cake!*"

"What will we do with so many cakes?" Helen asked.

"I asked my mother that same question. She guessed your parents probably donated them to their church. Let's call the pastor and see how they can be distributed. Tomorrow is Palm Sunday, so we will have time to do the work. Then we can donate them in your Mom and Dad's memory."

Aunt Edna and Uncle Theo's home was filled with laughter and happiness. My mother brought her recipes and we learned to 'cream' ingredients. She bought us aprons with yellow tulips and we covered them with flour and good intentions. With one mixer, one oven, and one sink we mixed, baked, and cleaned.

Dad and Michael arrived and I served the lamb cake. Everyone laughed in unison and said, "She cut the cake! She cut the cake! She cut the cake!" We raised our coffee mugs and toasted Aunt Edna and Uncle Theo.

"May they rest in peace and enjoy our handiwork."

Passions

BEES SWARMED AROUND OUR FOUR-YEAR-OLD GRAND-
daughter's lunch as she sat with us on the deck one clear June afternoon. Our pleasant conversation was suddenly interrupted when she ran into the house, crying and saying, "Bees, Mommy. Bees are out there!"

Years ago my husband had wanted to convert this space into a sunroom. I did not agree, until now. Later, as our daughter and her family pulled off the driveway, we waved good-by and I said to him, "Remember that sunroom you wanted to build over the deck?" He did and smiled. As we watched their car pass out of view, he said, "Doesn't have anything to do with bees scaring our granddaughter does it?"

The room, late in becoming one, had been unplanned and therefore not done. My husband had always seen it as it should be. He had been patient, but once consent was given, a comfortable room came to be in three weeks.

And now here I sit, its fourth summer, enjoying the view of my garden through large windows. Nature has decided to add its own contributions, exceeding my expectations with its own design. Like my husband, the garden could be patient for only so long.

Stacked-stone walls curve in small terraced layers defining a small hill; a clean edge of lush grass meets meandering borders of perennials; a small fish pond with a flagstone path leads to Japanese wooden benches made by the skilled hands of my husband. The ferns spilling over the stone walls are confined to their homes, but not for long. They thrive and demand attention and soon, very soon, for more space. The perennials have scattered seeds here and there, adding to the effect I cherish—flowers competing for space, with no soil to be seen as greenery fills all voids with varying heights that slide from highs to lows like waves of water in slow motion. The garden had been wildly transformed from a planned space into a random embellishment by nature and time.

The passion vines too reject all boundaries and follow their own course. It is their nature to fix things—to do what even a seasoned gardener cannot foresee. I will be forever grateful to them for their unique contribution to the sunroom. It happened so quickly I barely noticed until one hot summer morning when sunlight became filtered by their green leafiness covering the screens. A layer of coolness over the windows grew with differing degrees of wildness allowing me to feel as if I lived within a tree. The vine had used the screen to wrap its tendrils in a time-lapsed, Kudzu kind of energy and provided shade for human dwellers. Well, that and an exquisite view. If only I knew, years ago, I would not have hesitated for our sunroom has become a unique 'living' room.

Gauguin would have painted passion vine flowers as fabric draped upon a beautiful dark-skinned woman who seemed captivated by the mango she held. Georgia O'Keeffe would have been inspired to paint the blossom so large that the borders of her canvas could not contain it. And Picasso, during his period of Cubism, would have designed angled formations based on the flower's intricate layers.

Me? I was inclined to recline! From an old wicker chaise near these windows, I studied the passion vines and promised to hold their beauty in my memory forever. I tend to marvel at little things. I followed the lashing tendrils twisting into the screen, how they turn, say "oops" when they meet their cousins and intertwine with them before agreeing on a spot upon which to anchor. They are thinking, *How very kind this trellis is to allow us so many choices*! I am thinking, *My husband, the practical one, is going to be upset when he sees what nature has wrought upon the screens.*

Summer progresses and the vines decide to enter the sunroom by way of the door. Kicking them back did not hurt their feelings. They can be persistent in attempts to acquire more territory and are disappointed to learn I will not surrender. I would love too, but others would object and call me silly. They retreat, return to the outdoors and twine their way along the deck boards to cling and ensnare the legs of the chairs.

A visit from elderly aunts proved just how sociable these plants can be. As we all enjoyed a July afternoon on the deck, the aunts paid proper homage to the garden and, of course, the vines—which they carefully considered before sitting down. These plants are not subtle and, therefore, declared their attitude with a jungle's vengeance. One aunt, a loud, boisterous type, who I always enjoyed, was both amused and annoyed by them. As if to make nice, like a cat that continues to pester the only non-cat person in the group, the vines decided her leg looked promising. Wanting to be part of the festivities, one long stem seemed to accidentally fall from the wall near the door and behind her chair, resting at the back of her shoe. No one noticed but me because I am so aware of their habits. It wasn't long before her hand flicked at her ankle in between breaths in her conversation. Then losing patience with something so bothersome, she blurted out after noticing my twisting friends under her chair, "What the hell is going on?" My sweet aunt knew better than to stomp them into the boards, as would have been her nature to do, because she is a good and proper guest of a passionate gardener.

The passion vine describes me—changing directions as I leave one stage of life and advance to the next, adapting to suit a change of mood, or acting on impulse, an unplanned vision.

Inspired by the vines, I decided to dramatize the shade area which starts at the side gate near a sidewalk that eventually turns and gives a view of the entire yard from a good vantage point. Coming through the wooden gate, visitors will now appreciate Ostrich Fern clusters along with Japanese Painted Ferns. One tall, green and feathery: the other compact, deep textured with varying ranges of color from silvery areas to bold deep purple.

Plan, read, purchase, share, dig, plant, water, photograph—the ultimate gardener's thrill while waiting for the garden to once again design itself if given the freedom. I allow it, encourage the alterations to one person's idea. I want the viewer of this space to contemplate, to read the lyrical notes of the various flowerbeds, the rhythm of time passing, the promise of another spring.

Each morning, still in slippers and kimono robe, I stroll my small Eden to see what has changed since the previous day. I remember and note these in my mind. They may require my attention later. I deadhead the daisies, my daughter's favorite flower. I have put them in her bedroom from the time she was born until the day she married and carried a lush bouquet of them down the aisle of our small church. She had told me, "Mom, this will always be my favorite flower. Thanks to you, I grew up with daisies in my bedroom."

I walk the small path, pass the Japanese benches, and onto a large stepping stone by the pond where flashing scales of orange, white, silver, and blue disrupt the water with the anticipation of being fed.

The goldfish have had their babies, all black at this stage, camouflaged so as not to be eaten by their relatives in the pond. They wait nearby, often below a large fish, hoping to catch the floating leftovers spit out of their mouths when one's eyes are bigger than their tummy. The famished fish feed on large pieces, trying to get too much of a good thing. Their frenzied feeding time is a favorite part of my day and I will sit and enjoy until all are sated and ready for the next event: the pond becomes still once again, fins barely move and the fish appear to be resting!

I remember buying the first of them years ago. "Not interested in our beautiful Koi fish?" asked the young salesperson. One six inch Koi can cost $140-$160. Multicolored goldfish the same size, including the graceful fantails, cost $12. A koi pond, because of the cost, would have to be protected from hunting predators with a net covering. This, to me, inhibits meaning—it is no longer a pond, free and open to a variety of wildlife. With reeds, seagrasses and floating Hyacinths, I prefer to have protective areas for the fish to hide. Yes, raccoons have visited and left behind large snail shells and wet footprints. Herons have dined at the pond, and our Mama Cat has tried, failed and admitted defeat.

The passion vine is on the other side of the pond and it cascades, falling like water six feet down where it puddles at the edge of the water. In late summer it is weighed down by the passion flower's fruit. Sometimes as I stand inside the sunroom, I observe performances occurring around the water. From the vine-covered window, I spy and am close enough to see the fine, white feathers around the heron's eye and Mama Cat's whiskers twitching, preparing to pounce as she holds her paw over the water, waiting to strike. Thirsty opossums and rabbits have found their way to the trickling sound. Striped corn snakes have dozed on the warm rocks. Once, a Pileated Woodpecker came to drink, strolled around and was in no hurry to leave.

Big Blue is the oldest fish in the pond. One morning, she lay near the top of the water, barely moving, listless and not responding. My son heard my words of concern as I talked to the fish, came to me and placed his hand in the pond and under Big Blue. Then he slowly moved her through the water, back and forth, for several moments. He said, "CPR for a fish; I'm getting oxygen to pass through her gills." We watched and waited. Hoped. Waited. A stirring occurred, then Big Blue dashed from his hand and disappeared into the pond.

"Where did you learn that?" I asked somewhat surprised. I was doubtful. I was wrong. I was delighted!

"I didn't learn it. I was guessing about what to do and it seemed the most logical. So glad it worked, Mom."

In the northwest corner of the yard stands a potting shed made of red barn siding. A large space on the side of it is covered with an overhead trellis upon which Clematis paniculata draws the attention of every visitor as they turn the corner leading from the side gate. The leaves are shiny, the texture of leather. Their exquisite emerald green color offers a contrast for the thousands of dainty, white, star-shaped blossoms. This is the gift that keeps on giving with a mixture of honey and vanilla fragrances and as a nesting spot for Robins. Under this ceiling of growth is my sturdy potting table with shelves in convenient places. The garden hose is inches away, the compost pile is by the hose and two steps lead up a small hill to my reading deck which runs the length of the shed's upper structure. It is a private place from where I can see my carpet of Daylilies and no one can see me. It is not easy to concentrate on my book with so many distractions like hummingbirds and butterflies. But I manage.

Another visitor to my garden was one I will always remember with fondness—a six-foot, thick-bodied-black snake asleep among the Sweet Woodruff. Her blackness, her stillness, struck me as a most beautiful, rare event. With my finger, I slowly traced the coolness of her body. She did not stir, but my heart did. Next, my finger marked a longer length with a slight reaction from the snake— her life, her awakening, and then her disappearance into the damp undergrowth.

At the compost pile, I found she left me a gift. As I lifted the heavy, black tarp I saw many small, white, rubbery-to-the-touch eggs. Some of the baby snakes had hatched. Many scattered eggs displayed movement within them. One had begun the work of escaping its egg. Not yet the free creature it would soon become, it struggled until I moved my finger closer to its black thread-thin body. Pulling itself into an upright threatening position, the small head darted backward then lunged at me and thrust its forked tongue at danger. I withdrew my finger and smiled.

Crossing the moist grass, I placed my coffee down on a rocky ledge to enjoy my aromatics. They require two hands, like praying. I rubbed the leaves of Rosemary. Released the scent. Breathed it. Next, the Lemon Balm, then Basil. Every day should begin with the fragrance of herbs or flowers. It will improve one's attitude. It is a ritual I promote.

The garden is a force and I become indulgent to its whims and bow before it, thankful for a different point of view, the insight of Mother Earth.

Days are cooling and nights are longer: time for indoor passions like reading and writing. Adieu, my passion vines, my friends. It is November, but still they look pleased. My heart applauds their reluctance to be submissive to nature's clock.

So like myself.

Parts
of Me

CHAPTER 1

Anticipating

THE WORLD WILL NOT EXIST AFTER TODAY.

I am burdened by an awareness of impending doom upon awakening from a disturbing sleep. The nightmare moved with me from sleeping to waking. A hot shower did nothing to cleanse away the panic. Anxiety hovered. My eyes searched for clues, my ears pricked for warnings. Disaster of some kind? Floods, fires, riots? No, worse. Final, over, no more, nothing, gone and hopeless, helpless.

How will the end of us present itself?

The sunshine casts a shadows from the blinds onto the floor. Normal… it happens, it is predictable; I am disturbed by it. Given my fear, nothing should be ordinary.

To me it was a fact—*the world will not exist after today.*

And I wondered if anyone else knew.

I heard the muffled babble of television in the living room as Lewis, my teenage son, eats his cereal. I try to balance the tightening in my chest and the dread in my nerve endings with his usual morning routine. How did I come to know the world would end? What should I do?

Planning was of no use; I cannot prevent the inevitable. I envision the event occurring soon, this morning perhaps. Maybe the next minute. I brace myself. I will fight my fear and my children must not know.

The commentators' voices from the TV are normal, citing traffic slow-downs on main roads into downtown. *No alerts, mass evacuation notices, public-service announcements?*

I gaze at Lewis, walk over and kiss the top of his head. He ignores me, rubs the spot where my kiss had been and continues eating and watching. He suspects nothing. He is innocent.

Lewis grabs his backpack, heads for the door and says, "See you later, Mom."

I wish that were true, my son.

"Lewis, wait," I say and hug him tightly. I give him money for ice cream, thinking he will not have time to spend it. Then quickly, protectively, rethinking, I pray he will.

Emerging from our high rise into a sunny day, I feel relieved to be part of the morning's mundane surroundings. The whining of a garbage truck in the distance, the slap of a paper being delivered to the sidewalk and an approaching school bus are cause for celebration. Morning rituals on a normal day. Glancing skyward, I tighten my fists at the absence of birds fluttering about the large trees. *Where is the morning chorus from the mockingbirds?*

There are fewer cars on the road, so driving across to the gas station was much easier. Usually, this would have pleased me. Today, it made me suspicious.

The coffee machine is by a large window, overlooking the pumps. As I stir artificial every things into the hot brew, I watch a middle-aged man fill his car with gas. Glancing up, he sees me at the window. What he did next made me realize that, yes, others know and he perceived my knowing, my loneliness, and my search for confirmation. Keeping his eyes locked on mine, he removes his credit card from the pump, looks at it briefly, then back at me; he flips it over his shoulder. Our eyes are caught in a maddening grip of the death and destruction *we* foresee. The card is caught by the breeze of the passing traffic, twirls briefly with the sun catching the hologram and finds its way into the sewer. With a resigned look on his face, and a shrug of his shoulders, he broke his stare, got into his car and eased slowly into the traffic.

I am awestruck. Hot coffee splashes as my hand trembles.

Well, then, that's it. Acceptance. Resignation. He knows what I know and has not a clue, like me, what to do about it.

His eyes said, *"Why make others miserable? Secret, keep it a secret."*

Then again, who could we tell? Who would believe us? What is our proof? It is close to becoming a reality and preparations would not matter.

With whatever time is left, I must see my daughter, Alice, who was picked up earlier for all-day field events at her elementary school. My cell phone will ring soon asking why I am I late for a scheduled meeting. I remove it, turn it off and throw it into a recycling bin. I am focused, and like that car easing into traffic, I will ease into the time that remains and make good use of it.

The schoolyard is bustling with sounds of happiness. I search the sky for a hint of calamity as I study the faces of youngsters along the perimeter of the field. Halfway around, my palms sweaty and my breathing shallow, I quicken my pace. I smell danger. A cocker spaniel breaks from its leash and runs yelping as if in pain. Another dog does the same as both owners dash after them. Urgency replaces my pretend calmness. The breeze stops. Quiet, stillness. Parents cheer and the noise is welcoming, normal, but I cannot smile. Birds gather on the horizon, hundreds of them fly with abandon, wildly changing directions.

Where is my child? Where is Alice?

A breeze stirs, then increases, kicking up dust on the softball diamond. A dark cloud surfaces on the horizon and moves toward the sun.

"Alice, Alice, Alice," my mind screams.

"Alice, Alice, Alice!" My voice echoes in my ears as people turn towards me.

My eyes dart about as children sip power drinks, pat teammates on the back and cheer for events taking place on the field. I am dizzy and stumble, catching myself, then grabbing a nearby bench. People notice me, nod their heads, and whisper to each other.

Over my right shoulder and behind me, I see a blue baseball cap covering the eyes of a full-cheeked child with long, wispy, blonde hair held back in a ponytail. Ever so slowly, I reach out my hand to raise her face while whispering, "Alice?" The child steps back into her mother who glares at me. The child's questioning eyes meet my hopeful ones and in that second my world ends. Her mother protectively steps between us and asks, "Are you ok? You're acting strange. What is wrong?"

"Everything is wrong," I say.

An eerie whiteness silently envelops the area. People pause, seem confused, search the crowd for reassurance that everything is normal. They find no comfort. Has time stopped? Or is about to? The crack of the bat draws everyone's attention to the young child running the bases. The crowd yells with encouragement. Except for a few like me who seem unable to move.

A slight touch at my elbow and a man's whisper. "You know, don't you?" the tall stranger asks. "I've been watching you and I can tell that you know." He grasps my hand firmly. I have no voice…cannot speak, cannot scream.

CHAPTER 2

Participating

I AM GONE, EMPTIED AND DISPERSED, EXPERIENCING EVENTS I do not know or understand. Surrounded by darkness with small bursts of light, pieces of me—small, unidentified particles—drift in slow waves in what could be a nightmare in a nighttime sky. Am I rising then falling, turning then tumbling, relaxed then astonished? If this is what *I* have become, are there parts of others being carried along on a galactic current? Does a former nature of *us* linger in this cosmic dust catching the light of the universe? I want to connect to their parts. Tranquility coils then hovers above me. Is their a pondering of our circumstances? Our energies are not mindless—I am aware of us taking pleasure in this moment with a sense of wonder surrounded by the light and the dark. Has something ended or has it just begun?

I am working to make sense of this experiment. Will my splintered self require a combined energy of the others to accept something new? Are we a group? Have I been here forever? Or was I, were we, the others, not here? Is there a future? Thoughts come quickly, a mental grid and how do I know these words? The gathering in, reaping ideas from a surge of energy, ever faster and more powerful twists, then a new word: past—was there a past—what past or passed?

I am a shadow in time and place, uniting with a universe that does not resist my attempts to belong. I...we exist. We are real. I feel I am. I do what I can to sustain physical and mental awareness, hoping I can **be**. I sense that thousands of forever fragments are attempting to pull themselves, itself, together. I propel toward particles in a whirling spectacle, speeding across a starless sky. My musing makes me joyful! I am advancing toward **being** again, maybe.

CHAPTER 3

Reflecting

———————

IMPRESSIONS SLASH THROUGH ME, COMMINGLED ELEMENTS of **becoming**, slivers moving so rapidly that they dissolve. Was I thinking, asking, or concluding? Components surfing the galaxy, reacting, waking to a nocturnal consciousness in an expanse of wonderment.

Can I pull myself together? Do I want to? If only I knew…if only they knew…